Then he saw her.

She gazed unblinkingly back at him, and if the eyes were the window to the soul these eyes had the curtains open, the bed unmade and a woman lying naked, all hot and flushed and bothered. And waiting.

For him.

Oh, yeah, this was enough to take his mind off the team.

Big blue eyes, round cheeks dusted with rosy colour and a ruby curve of a mouth that made her look on the verge of a smile. He found his own mouth reluctantly returning that smile. She had a subtle fullness to her face that made him unaccountably think of Renaissance Madonnas.

She was a stunningly beautiful girl. In any era.

For a moment he allowed himself the fantasy of having her brought up to his suite. He'd have her run that accent over him on her knees, bury his hands in that thick dark hair. He'd...

...lost his goddamned mind.

Lucy Ellis has four loves in life: books, expensive lingerie, vintage films and big, gorgeous men who have to duck going through doorways. Weaving aspects of them into her fiction is the best part of being a romance writer. Lucy lives in a small cottage in the foothills outside Melbourne.

Recent titles by the same author:

UNTOUCHED BY HIS DIAMONDS
INNOCENT IN THE IVORY TOWER

**Did you know these are also available as eBooks?
Visit www.millsandboon.co.uk**

THE MAN SHE SHOULDN'T CRAVE

BY
LUCY ELLIS

First published in Great Britain 2012
by Mills & Boon, an imprint of Harlequin (UK) Limited.
Harlequin (UK) Limited, Eton House, 18-24 Paradise Road,
Richmond, Surrey TW9 1SR

© Lucy Ellis 2012

ISBN: 978 0 263 22767 3

Harlequin (UK) policy is to use papers that are natural, renewable and recyclable products and made from wood grown in sustainable forests. The logging and manufacturing process conform to the legal environmental regulations of the country of origin.

Printed and bound in Great Britain

THE MAN SHE SHOULDN'T CRAVE

For Charlotte

CHAPTER ONE

SHE'D come all the way to Toronto to find herself a man. Just not this man.

Shoot! She hoped it wasn't this man.

Yet, unable to help herself, Rose drank him in—along with every other woman in the room.

Broad, high cheekbones, long straight nose, wide sullen mouth and deepset eyes the colour of a night sky. His bored expression only highlighted the male beauty of his face. Undeniably the gene pool had blessed him. He stood far over six feet, his lean, muscular body clad in expensive dark threads that remained faithful to the strength of him and drew Rose's attention to how essentially different the male body was from the female.

As if she'd needed reminding, but this man just seemed to be in your face about it.

It wasn't as if he didn't have competition. A huddle of gorgeous young men, shifting in their suits, jostled either side of him. They were talking amongst themselves, one of them smirking at the cameras, another looking a little shy.

Rose could feel her face becoming flushed, but this wasn't the moment to suffer an attack of nerves. She'd known what she was getting into when she'd first spotted the Wolves' visit to Toronto in the daily newspaper. It was so high-profile it had leapt out of the sports section altogether and landed on 'look at me' page three along with a grainy photo of a couple of the team's stars.

Rose cared about sport about as much as she was interested in stock prices, but what the featured article had very clearly told her was other women *did* care. They cared a great deal. Not about the sport—that was all statistics and injuries, sweat and testosterone. No, women were interested in what all red-blooded females the world over paid attention to: a good-looking man with a honed body who knew how to use it.

The Wolves had that in spades, as well as the addition of some very high-profile players. And then there was that Russian thing they had going on. Melancholy eyes and high broad cheekbones, and rich dark accents that rolled *r*'s like Formula One™-tuned tyres—hard and fast into the corners.

Rose liked to think she knew exactly what women wanted. She liked to think she was an expert. She—and the bank that held her loan—was depending on her expertise.

She wanted to prove to the world—or perhaps only to metropolitan Toronto—that she knew what women wanted in a man and how to get it.

Except she hadn't reckoned on *this* man. He was talking quietly to the guy at his side, but his gaze kept sweeping the room, bored, moody.

Simmering, Rose decided, fanning herself with the programme the girl at the door had shoved into her unresisting hand.

It seemed the city's press had turned up to hear what these young, built Russian athletes, uncomfortable in their suits, had to say. The Russian national ice hockey team was dominant in the sport, but this Siberian team had all the glamour of its owner, Plato Kuragin, whose personal wealth and notorious reputation existed apart from the team. With him was a former national team coach but not, Rose noted, the couple of players—twin brothers—the NHL here in Canada were keen to poach. More star Russian athletes had come out of the Wolves team than any other in the country.

Not that Rose cared—and she knew that neither did any of the other women in the room if they were honest. What mattered was that the guys were all *hot*. This press jaunt wasn't about sport. It was about sex. Sex sold everything nowadays.

Women wanted them. Men wanted to be like them. She wanted a couple of ice hockey players to do a guest spot for her dating agency. It was publicity money couldn't buy, and as she didn't have very much money she intended to use charm to get what she wanted. A Southern woman's greatest asset.

It was why she hadn't approached the Wolves management team with her request. She had decided to put her man-handling skills to the ultimate test.

Except the best of the bunch, Mr Tall, Bored and Built, was the one footing the bill, and Rose suddenly knew she was in a lot of trouble—because feminine instinct told her Plato Kuragin wasn't a man she could handle. At all.

Rose had never seen a man less in need of a dating agency. He was built like an athlete, but everything about him asserted authority and power. She didn't have to be told who he was. Oh, yes, this was the guy who would cause her some trouble.

Well, her daddy hadn't raised a quitter, and that was why she was standing here in the middle of a media scrum in Toronto's Dorrington Hotel with that sinking feeling in the pit of her stomach.

People were firing questions at him in Russian and English, and although she didn't understand much of it she heard every word said in the deep, deliberate voice from up front. Wanting to get another look at him, Rose shuffled sideways in an effort to detach herself from the scrum.

'Pardon. Sorry. Just a sec—sorry.'

This wasn't strictly necessary—in fact understated to the point of invisible was supposed to be her *modus operandi*—but she now had an uninterrupted view. A daunting view.

Thank God he wasn't in her plan. She could not possibly approach this man.

And then she realised he'd stopped speaking. He was looking at her. His eyes, so deep and intense in their regard, were riveted on hers, and what she saw in them had a direct effect on her breathing. As in it completely stopped.

He angled his big muscular body towards her and what broke the spell, Rose realised, was the fact that she'd stepped towards *him*. Just fractionally, but clearly enough for him to notice.

Also enough to step on the back of the shoe of the woman in front of her, who said something rude. And then the facilitator standing on the podium made a gesture towards her and said, *'Angliski?* English?'

A microphone was shoved in front of her face. Rose looked down at it and back up into those spectacular, mesmerising eyes that were… Why was he looking at her like that?

Ask a question, Rose. He wants you to ask him a question.

Her throat, already dry and unaccountably scratchy, was constricted. She ran her tongue along her bottom lip. From somewhere her voice came, all high and breathy and really, really Texan.

'Are y'all single?'

CHAPTER TWO

PLATO was not a fan of the media, but he knew how to play their game. You turned up; you used the publicity; you told them nothing.

Not that it would stop the tabloid reports, but it might deflect somewhat from the constant stream of drivel emanating from his last five-minute girlfriend about blondes and orgies on super-yachts. The bath of vintage champagne a burlesque dancer was supposed to have performed in at his recent twenty-eighth birthday celebration was the most current story doing the rounds. Yet, despite that last report actually being true, there was something belittling about seeing it all strung out like so many coloured lights—as if in the end this was his net worth. Lurid entertainment for the masses.

His media profile, however, helped out the team, and he had turned up today to give the coach and the boys the benefit of his press exposure.

It was a simple meet-and-greet before the match, but his mind was elsewhere. He'd spent this morning at a local gaol as his lawyers went through the paperwork to get two of his best players out of the cells. They were both currently holed up in a hotel room with Security. He didn't trust them on their own. But it was only a matter of time before the story broke.

For the time being, though, he needed to keep a cap on it.

Then he saw her.

She gazed unblinkingly back at him, and if eyes were the

windows to the soul these eyes had the curtains wide open, the bed unmade and a woman lying bare naked, all hot and flushed and bothered. And waiting.

For him.

Oh, yeah, this was enough to take his mind off the team.

Big blue eyes, round cheeks dusted with rosy colour, and a ruby curve of a mouth that made her look on the verge of a smile. He catalogued every one of her attributes and found his own mouth predictably returning that smile. Until this moment he'd had nothing to smile about all day. Things had just turned around.

Plato found himself standing a little straighter, with purpose edging back his shoulders. She was an angel, he thought, amused at his own susceptibility. The subtle fullness of her face made him unaccountably think of Renaissance Madonnas.

Da, a stunningly beautiful girl. In any era.

Aware she had completely stolen away his attention from the event at hand, he asked for her question.

For a moment her blank expression had him about to redirect to someone else, but then the little goddess licked her sweet ruby lips, opened her mouth, and asked the only question that needed no answer.

The entire world knew he was single.

At this moment, thanks to the disgruntled ex-girlfriend, he was possibly the most single man on the planet.

As the room reacted with laughter the girl, goal achieved, gazed levelly back at him.

Wealth and good-looks had given him rock star privileges when it came to women—privileges he was no longer so quick to indulge in. But she was not to know that. For a moment he allowed himself the fantasy of having her brought up to his suite. He'd have her run that accent over him on her knees, bury his hands in that thick dark hair. He'd…

…lost his goddamned mind.

Another question came at him. This time something about the national team. He could answer that in his sleep—which was just as well because Blue Eyes was making her way to the front of the room and she had taken his full attention with her.

She was bold. He had to give her that. A member of his security team intercepted her, and from the corner of his eye he watched as she remonstrated with the man.

Then a sharp-eyed rep from the *Moscow Times* lifted a hand, and the questions zeroed in on the rumour that Sasha Rykov would be signing with a Canadian team. Plato's attention swerved back to doing an effective job of spin to keep the question at the forefront of everyone's mind. As long as the press were asking about Rykov they wouldn't be asking any uncomfortable questions about the absence of two of their best players.

The coach, Anatole Medvedev, fielded the next question, and after several more it was meet-and-greet time. He made it a practice to keep moving in these situations, keeping any interaction brief. There were corporate sponsors and a lot of journalists. He'd keep his eyes on the boys. A few of them were still wet behind the ears, but the language barrier would solve any concerns about an info leak.

Blue Eyes had vanished, taking his sexual fantasy with her.

Feeling a little shaky after her encounter with the big, bad boss of the Wolves, Rose looked around the room, knowing it was better to get this done fast—kind of like pulling a tooth. All she needed was two definite takers.

It crossed her mind that it still wasn't too late. She could walk out of here, go home, forget about the publicity. She was uncomfortably aware her behaviour could be perceived as a little underhand. But this was about more than her business. It was about the women's shelter where she volunteered, and where she hoped to be able to offer more than just her professional counsel. If Date with Destiny was the success she hoped it could be, there was a real chance come the end of the year, when the lease on the shelter came up, that they could move to larger, better premises.

And there was no way she was going to get even one of these players on side through legitimate avenues. She'd tried. No one would speak to her.

On a less important but personal level, today was also about firming up her confidence in herself. If she could do this—if she could take on an entire Russian ice hockey team with a bit of charm and a line of chat—she could finally put the past into a box and ship it to Utah. She was done with being that unhappy, humiliated girl who had fled Houston two years ago.

She spotted a couple of team members gripping wineglasses like life jackets, clearly cut off by the language barrier. They would have been easy pickings—they reminded her of herself once—but they weren't the ones she wanted. She wanted confident, a bit brash, hard to pin down. Those were the guys who would sell her business.

It was absurd, but it was human nature. You always wanted what you couldn't have. A guy who had the world at his feet, who could have any woman, who could walk away at any time, was not long-term material. That was certainly not the type of guy she wanted on her books. Too much hard work.

But they were perfect for publicity purposes.

She just realised she'd described Plato Kuragin to a tee. Not that she would be approaching *him* any time soon. She was confident, but she wasn't delusional.

Her plan was to send a couple of these hockey boys out on dates, add a film crew to the mix, and pull in a favour with a local TV producer who was the friend of a friend who had assured her a spot if she could pull it off.

Now she only had to find a couple of photogenic specimens and run her little pick-up spiel by them.

She had a lot of competition. There were some seriously gorgeous women here. But attracting a man's attention had less to do with looks and more to do with confidence—and it helped to have a plan.

She fixed herself in front of the dark-haired athlete she'd seen earlier, smirking for the press corps.

'Oh, my, nobody move!' She made a helpless gesture, lifted her gaze so that they made definite eye contact, and then dropped to her knees. 'My contact lens!' she wailed.

The guy dropped to his haunches and cast his gaze around on the floor—but mainly had a good long look at the shape of her bottom and thighs outlined by her crouching position. A few minutes of pointless searching and she was coming to her feet and holding out her hand.

'Rose.'

'Sasha.'

She was aware they were being surreptitiously watched by a couple of women, and Rose knew she'd made a good choice. She thanked him, made sure she kept eye contact because guys liked confidence, bemoaned how fuzzy the world suddenly looked and asked him how he was enjoying Toronto.

It only took a few minutes before she had his vital statistics: enthusiastic, a bit dull, and possessing less confidence around women than his outer swagger would suggest. But he had the face of an angel. It wasn't hard to scrawl her cell number on his hand, and she added her name: 'Rose'. He didn't look bright enough to remember it if she simply left her trademark drawing of the flower.

It was her signature strategy. Handing out business cards would be intimidating to some of these boys, and likely to go straight into the bin. The coy girl who pressed ink to their palm was going to be remembered.

Everyone was sceptical about a young woman setting up her first business on such a flimsy premise as matchmaking, but Rose knew her youth was on her side. She came across as unthreatening, unserious, and to some of these men as a bit of harmless fun. The fact she had been doing this since she was eight years old and considered herself an old hand at it was her secret weapon.

After all, she had managed to find a wife for her father, and two of her four brothers, and several of her girlfriends were happily settled with men Rose had helped them land.

It was a little different when *she* was doing the landing, keeping a smile on her face despite the bite of her heels and the uncomfortable warmth of her wool suit, and every time she approached a new face her heart began to pound.

Today was all about Date with Destiny, but in the days leading up to this, as she'd formulated her plan, something else had been growing alongside it. Right now it was gnawing at her, and if she was honest with herself turning up today was about much more than business. There was a recklessness in choosing to go this route that turned it into the bold move she needed to make. She had played it safe for four years under the watchful eyes of her fiancé's ambitious family, and where had that got her? What did it say about her matchmaking skills when she was twenty-six and still single…?

No, she was going to put herself on the line—for the business but more importantly for herself—and if pesky doubts were already crowding in she'd just ignore them.

But so far, so good, and she hoped the results would be at least one phone call later today. Then she could make her approach.

Plato watched as Blue Eyes cut a swathe through his boys. Every time he looked around she was with a different player. What in the hell was she up to? Although given a couple of seconds he could guess.

He was on the move away from the CEO of one of the brands the boys would be wearing on their shirts on Saturday when he heard a soft, twangy 'Hey…' Against his better judgement he halted, turned, made a gesture to his security officer, who was barring her path.

A big smile crossed her lovely face and up came some serious dimples. He hadn't expected those. He *had* expected the approach, however.

He could see all of her now. She was wearing a double-breasted blue and black plaid wool jacket and a knee-length matching fitted skirt. A pair of long shapely legs in black tights plunged down into aqua coloured high heels. Vaguely he understood this was some form of retro fashion statement. Her dark hair was pulled back severely from her face, but it only served to draw attention to those big eyes, that lush mouth, the slightly upturned nose and the apple-round curve of her cheeks and gently rounded chin, echoing the curves below.

And she had some serious curves. She was all woman.

'Y'all didn't answer my question,' she said brightly.

This was going to kill him. 'Not as single as you'd probably like, *detka*,' he said.

She crossed the space between them.

'I get that you probably don't want to talk right now,' she said rapidly.

Up close, she was not quite as confident as she had initially appeared. Her gaze cut shyly away as he looked down at her, but instinct and experience with women told him it was a calculated gesture.

She looked back up, a determined glint in her eyes, and waved a gold pen. 'Can I give you my cell number?'

He chuckled and reluctantly turned away. She was beautiful *and* persistent.

To his surprise he felt her hand close over his forearm. If she'd been a man his security detail would have been all over her, but they'd seen the exchange. Women approached him all the time. He was unfailingly polite, but definite. He did the chasing.

'Please,' she said, flashing those dimples as if she wasn't accosting the man everyone in this room wanted to talk to but just a random guy in the street.

She took his hand and he let her, curious to see what she was up to. Her touch was gentle, as soft and female as the rest of her looked.

She waved the pen. 'Promise not to wash it off.'

He allowed her to ink several digits across his palm.

'My name is Rose Harkness,' she said sweetly, suddenly

all eyes and sincerity, 'and I've got a business proposition for you. Call me.'

Business proposition? Was that what they were calling it these days?

He didn't bother to glance at the number, but he did take a last look at what he was leaving behind. A year ago he might have taken her up on the offer, and even now he was tempted to take her along with him. She ticked all the boxes: beautiful, built, no strings. But he wasn't doing one-nighters with women any more, and he wasn't letting her ricochet through his team either. He shrugged, gave her a wink and kept moving.

As he stepped into the service elevator with the Wolves coach, Anatole Medvedev, and his head of security, he said, 'Make sure that woman is turned out of the hotel. She's got an agenda.'

That went well, thought Rose. At least she'd got all her lines out. For a moment her vocal cords had seized up when Plato Kuragin had run his critical gaze over her. A man who dated supermodels and actresses and other women without bottoms to speak of. She'd been too overwhelmed even to check his reaction. Yet she'd stood her ground, she'd run her line by him, and he'd seemed to enjoy it—although there was a fine line between an unusual approach and ending up sounding like a groupie.

The athletes had been easy—a couple a bit standoffish, but for the most part receptive, and they seemed like nice guys.

Plato Kuragin—he was something else entirely. She'd been high on confidence when she'd approached him, taken one look into those rain-over-stone dark grey eyes and lost the plot. Plato Kuragin was *not* going to line up to be Date with Destiny's poster-boy. No, she'd approached him because she could. Because she was a red-blooded woman and she couldn't resist.

Of all the monumentally stupid spur-of-the-moment decisions. She had come very close to blowing it, and she knew darn well why. Pesky hormones. But there was also this irresistible pull to behave a little recklessly. She'd approached the players for the business, but she'd fronted up to their big, bad boss because she *could*. Because the new Rose was all about being bold and brave.

Comfortably seated in the bar of the hotel, Rose took out her cell and set it down where she could see it. It was always possible one of the athletes would call her whilst she was still in the hotel. She hoped so. Then she could have the conversation on neutral ground. She ordered a soft drink and busied herself making notes on how she was going to sell Date with Destiny to her first caller.

Instead her pen began making circles on the page, and she found herself recalling how Plato Kuragin had smiled at her— as if she was the only woman in the room—and how imposing he was close up.

He had to be at least six foot six. She'd barely reached his chin in her heels, and the forearm she'd grasped had been twice as broad as her own, covered in golden hairs that glinted under the bright chandelier lights of the reception room. The callused, roughened palm she'd held could have enclosed her hand entirely. Those labourer's hands didn't fit the image she had of him as a playboy tycoon, with models—usually of the blonde Scandinavian kind—draped around his neck. That big, muscle-honed body didn't come from sitting behind a desk or lying on the deck of a super-yacht all day long. And it didn't come from a gym either. He looked like a guy who used his body.

Rose propped her elbows up on the table and planted her chin in her hands. She had plenty of time to contemplate that body…

'Excuse me, miss.'

Rose looked up to find two men in hotel uniforms standing over her. Her usual ready smile evaporated as she listened to their request that she leave the hotel.

'I beg your pardon?'

'You were observed accosting several of our visiting international guests earlier this evening. Mr Kuragin has personally requested your removal.'

Rose blinked. 'What? Why?'

An uneasy feeling slid down Rose's spine even as the man cleared his throat.

'Procurement is not something our hotel turns a blind eye to, madam.'

Rose's mouth fell open. 'You think I'm a *hooker*?'

After that there wasn't much conversation. Just a security officer marching her none too gently through the lobby.

Outside the light had started to dwindle and the sleet to fall. As Rose walked the four blocks to where she had left her car she tried not to take any of it personally. This wasn't about her; it was about the business.

Really, Rose? her conscience niggled. Because she knew it wasn't the whole truth of the matter. There was a fine line between being bold and behaving with reckless abandon, and she suspected she'd come down a little too heavily on the latter side.

Walking a little faster, she told herself she was new at putting herself out there. She was bound to make mistakes. Often being bold and brash meant you didn't get quite what you bargained for. She certainly hadn't banked on being evicted from the hotel for soliciting!

Not that she regretted one bit acting on her impulses for once. No, sirree. Playing it too careful had got her nowhere thus far. She folded her arms protectively around herself. Besides, you needed a thick skin in the service industry.

Except something hopeful had been lit inside her when Plato Kuragin had smiled at her. She'd got the erroneous impression he was interested. Which just showed how delusional she was.

Okay, it wasn't the worst thing that had ever happened to her. Although it was kind of disconcerting to discover that the only man you had met in for ever who got your pulse racing and your body temperature tipping over into tropical had assumed you were in a different kind of service industry, and informed the hotel management you were a hooker!

CHAPTER THREE

'HIYA, Rose, no date tonight?'

Her elderly neighbour in the adjoining townhouse on George Street greeted her at the gate. It was after six, and cold and dark, but Rita Padalecki had a small ageing dog who needed regular trips to the garden.

'No, Mrs Padalecki, not tonight.'

'I keep hoping for you, Rose.'

Rose smiled, opening her front door. She wondered what Mrs Padalecki would say if she told her she'd been turned out of a hotel tonight for procurement? She knew what her father and brothers would say. *You're packing up and coming back home.*

Fortunately her family didn't need to know any more than her sweet, elderly neighbour. No, refreshingly, she could keep that little blip on her radar to herself.

She headed upstairs, kicking off her heels as she dropped onto the end of her bed and fired up her laptop. She wanted to get this onto her blog before she turned in for the evening.

Met the Wolves ice hockey team today. Ladies, they are all single. Learned some curious facts about Russia, pucks and how to drink vodka. Unfortunately Grigori and Ivan Sazanov were in the land of the missing. If you see any gorgeous Russian men looking lost, send them our way. Study up on your ice hockey, girls.

She smiled at her own silliness and posted the photo she had taken of Sasha Rykov. She'd told him she wanted to use it on her blog and he'd shrugged and smiled. Then again, Plato Kuragin had shrugged and smiled—and look where that had left her. On the pavement with a scarlet letter on her back.

Right, that's enough. Forget Plato Kuragin. Remember how well the rest of the day went and give yourself props for fronting up and taking a chance.

She shut the lid on her laptop and padded off barefoot to run a bath.

Half an hour later Rose emerged into her bedroom, wet hair wrapped in a handtowel. She was too tired to prepare anything, so rang and ordered a pizza from her local, picking at the remains of a Danish she'd had this morning as she did so. Carrying a cold glass of white wine in one hand and a book in the other, she made herself comfortable on the sofa and kept her phone in sight. No bites yet, but she remained hopeful.

Plato skimmed the printout his security adviser had handed him.

'What in the hell is this?'

'Rose Red's blog. The woman you asked us to run a check on—Rose Harkness. This is what came up. She posted it thirty minutes ago.'

'Rose Red? What's that? Her working name?'

'She runs a website—a dating agency.'

Plato looked up swiftly. Was that what they were calling it nowadays? 'Do you have an address for her?'

'We do. How would you like it handled?'

Discreetly. For some reason his mind replayed the way she had cut her gaze away when she was speaking to him, as if shoring up her courage, and it interfered with his first thought which was to have his legal team make a threatening phone call.

'*Nyet*, I'll handle this myself. E-mail me the address. I take it she's in central Toronto?'

'The old district. Nice area.'

He didn't doubt that. There had been something classy about her. Less to do with the suit and more to do with the way she had infiltrated that room, sweet and sassy, but low-key. A woman with a mission but not drawing attention to herself.

He picked up the printout again. It was innocuous enough, but it drew attention to the very thing he didn't want questions about: the absence of the Sazanov brothers. Also, Anatole had told him she'd spoken to nearly all the boys and given them her number.

He should let Security deal with this. There was no reason for him to get involved…other than the smudged line of digits still faintly visible on his left hand, the invitation in her blue eyes and the unreasonable desire he still had to take her up on it.

He was in the Ferrari and driving downtown when he acknowledged that the shape of that ruby-red mouth and the promise in those baby blues had a little more to do with it. The sat nav took him to a quiet tree-lined street with traditional gabled townhouses close to the kerb. He didn't know what he'd expected, but it wasn't this. A residential home in a nice neighbourhood.

An elderly lady peered at him over the low railing fence as he strode up the path to the front door of number seventeen.

'She's home,' chirped the woman helpfully. 'And who are you, dear?'

Plato stopped, frowned. 'Plato Kuragin,' he said simply.

'Foreign,' said the woman. 'She's never had any foreign gents here before. When did you meet?'

When did they…? 'This afternoon,' he drawled. 'It's cold, madam, shouldn't you be inside?'

'It's Wiggles. He needs to do his business before bed. This afternoon, you say? Well, you're a quick worker. Mind you be good to her. She's a sweet girl, our Rose. I don't like this business she's in. I think it hardens a girl, makes her cynical.

I should have asked—are you a date or a client? It's confusing with her running the agency from home.'

Plato wasn't given a chance to reply as Wiggles chose that moment to come hurtling across the garden and into the house. Plato had a glimpse of something resembling a grey streak, and the elderly lady, with a little cry of surprise, vanished after him.

Plato rapped the lion's-head door knocker. Hard.

The light went on and the door opened, and for a moment Plato forgot what he was doing there, on a doorstep in an inner suburban neighbourhood of Toronto, chasing down a woman who might or might not be a lady of the night and being door-stepped by her elderly neighbour and a dog called Wiggles.

Texas Rose stood on the threshold in a red silk robe with definitely some serious black silk and lace something under-neath. Faint music he identified as Ravel's *Boléro* was coming from another room, and in the downlights of the hallway the interior of her home hinted at a cavern of sensual delight. But the comparisons with a bordello ended there.

Her head was wrapped in a white towel and her face was scrubbed bare, so that her nose looked a little pink, and she was holding out a twenty-dollar bill that retreated as she took in his presence.

'You're not pizza,' she said faintly.

'Nyet,' he said, wondering if the boys at the pizzeria threw dice to see which one got to deliver to Texas Rose. 'Can I come in?'

She gazed back at him, looking as flummoxed as he was feeling but no doubt for different reasons.

He had been expecting this, but also he hadn't. Hell, he didn't know *what* he'd expected. All he knew was that he should turn around right now, get back in his car and drive away, and forget this had ever happened.

Except in that moment her towel turban slipped and, de-spite her attempt to keep it in place, damp, dark hair spilled out. All of a sudden he became aware of her nipples peaking against soft fabric, and the stroke of her tongue along the inside of her bottom lip. It all seemed to happen at once and he stepped forward, definitely going in.

'I'm not sure this is a good idea,' she said, backing up.

'*Nyet,*' he agreed, 'it's probably a very bad idea.' He watched the outline of her breasts shift beneath that silk. She wasn't wearing a bra. His mind went blank. The most powerful surge of lust shot through him.

'Are you alone?'

'Yes. No.'

She was staring at him warily, and it took a moment for her alarm to penetrate his thick fog of desire. What in the *hell* was he doing?

'I'm here to speak to you,' he said, clearing his voice, as if that sorted it all out.

She looked so appalled by the idea that it brought him back to reality. 'Miss Harkness,' he said with exaggerated formality, 'you crashed that press conference today. We can either do this on the doorstep, or sitting down like a civilised man and woman.'

The tone of command seemed to do the trick.

'Where are my manners?' she said rapidly. 'Of course. Won't you come on in, Mr Kuragin?'

The sudden switch from open-mouthed alarm to Southern hospitality was too abrupt for his liking.

As was the sway of those hips as she preceded him down the narrow hall. He could see the outline of her bottom shifting under the silk, a little too wide and round for current fashion, but he had lost interest in contemporary standards of the female form the moment she opened that door. Texas Rose had one of those lush bodies found in paintings of nineteenth-century odalisques. He had a few of them hanging on the walls in his home in Moscow. Slender, but stacked in all the right places.

He followed her into a small front room from which the music was emanating. He noted the drawn drapes, the functional but pretty furniture, the place on the sofa where she had obviously been sitting: a red cashmere throw disturbed, a half-glass of wine, a book and a pair of wire-rimmed reading glasses. Not the accoutrements of a woman who was regularly entertaining men.

'Please sit down,' she said, with a degree of formality at odds with her *deshabillé* state.

He noted her cheeks were scorched red, and one of her hands was clenching at the ribbon tie that kept her robe vaguely cloaking what lay beneath: the full glory of those stupendous breasts.

'If you'll excuse me? I won't be a moment.'

'I don't excuse you, and I want you to sit down.' When she jumped he added, *'Now.'*

The bark in his voice had come from nowhere, but this woman and this routine she was performing was getting to him. Who in the hell did she think she was? Turning up at the Dorrington, making doe-eyes at the boys and then dragging him across town, offering up tantalising glimpses of a truly epic female body and then faking this *I must preserve my modesty* act...

Her eyes flew wide and her other hand darted up to crisscross her breasts with her arms. It was a classic 'woman in peril' gesture, and it almost convinced him he'd overreacted, was in fact completely in the wrong.

'I want to get changed, Mr Kuragin. And you're a guest in my house...'

'Nyet, I'm not one of your *guests*, Rose. Speaking of which— your neighbour was very informative.'

'Mrs Padalecki? You spoke to her?' Something in her expression eased a little.

'As I said, informative. You run your agency from your home?'

'Yes,' Rose said slowly, edging towards the sofa.

'You are zoned for this?'

'Zoned?'

He watched curiously as she made a snatch for the red cashmere throw and held it up under her chin, effectively shielding herself. He wanted to tell her it was unnecessary. He had no intention of sampling the merchandise. But that would have been a lie, he acknowledged ruefully. His intentions were being felt all too painfully—it was just he had no intention of acting on them.

'I am not familiar with the Canadian laws,' he said steadily, 'but that can be remedied. I could be your worst nightmare, Rose.'

All the colour that had been so charmingly lighting up her face drained away. 'If you don't get out of my house I'm calling the police.' Her voice faltered. 'Mrs Padalecki will call the police.'

'Your neighbour seemed to think I was a client…or a date. Sounds as if men are in and out of here all the time.'

He picked up the book lying on the table between them. *Madame Bovary.*

He frowned.

'Get out!' Her voice cracked and for the first time he noticed her hands were trembling.

'Sit down, Rose. I'm here to discuss your little foray into the world of ice hockey. You can either do it with me, or with my legal team.'

Her lashes fluttered. 'Your legal—legal team?' She sat down abruptly on the sofa. 'You're here to talk about what happened today?'

'*Da,*' he said brusquely, annoyed at how vulnerable she suddenly appeared as relief coloured her voice.

'Oh.' She released a breath. Her shoulders, however, remained stiff little jolts of wariness.

Plato glanced around the room. This wasn't a den of iniquity. It was a comfortable home. A woman's home. There were framed photographs on ledges, frilly-edged lamps, and a gorgeous girl huddled in a red cashmere throw gazing up at him as if he'd staged a home invasion.

It wasn't a familiar experience for him, but he finally acknowledged he might have overreacted. She swiped her bottom lip with that little pink tongue again and he had a fairly good idea *why* he'd overreacted. Sexual energy wasn't just moving at a rate of knots through his body, it was thrumming in the air between them. *Boléro*, reaching its crescendo even on a low volume, wasn't helping.

'Can you turn that off?' he growled.

She blinked rapidly, reaching across the table for the remote. The sudden silence was almost worse.

'Won't you sit down?' Rose said softly.

Da. Sit down. Don't loom over her. Keep this brief and to the point. Then get the hell out of here.

As he lowered his big body into a far too fragile armchair across from her she took the opportunity to push back some of the heavy, curling damp hair that was falling forward over her shoulder, drawing attention to the creaminess of her skin visible between the throw and her robe. Peignoir, he thought distractedly. That was what they were called, those flimsy little veils women wore to make men think about what was underneath. He didn't need help with that thinking. Those curves and hollows were burned into his retinas.

'If this is about what happened with Security I want you to know, Mr Kuragin, seeing you've already threatened me with legal action, I could sue *you* for defamation.'

'*Izvenitye*? Pardon?'

'You told the hotel security I was soliciting!'

He shrugged. 'Those are your words, Rose. I told my chief of security you had an agenda.'

As she grappled to come to terms with the fact that Plato Kuragin was in her house—*the* Plato Kuragin, of the killer looks, killer financial skills and, if the tabloids she'd skimmed through in her research were to believed, similarly honed skills with the opposite sex—Rose became aware right there and then she'd lost a little ground. She *did* have an agenda. She had quite a big agenda.

She just hadn't factored in this man taking any sort of interest in it. *But then you did target him too, Rose,* a little voice niggled. *And now this has happened and what are you going to do about it?*

It was just she'd never expected him in a million years to call. That he had turned up at her home was off the scale. But he was talking about legal teams and threatening legal action and…and he was looking at her mouth again. Did she have crumbs on her lips? She thought hungrily of the half-eaten Danish on her kitchen bench.

Aware her panic levels had dropped sufficiently for her to be thinking about food again, Rose wondered why she had thought Plato Kuragin had nefarious intentions.

It was the way he had stormed into her house, she reasoned, refusing to let her dress, welding those stunning dark eyes to her body as if heat-seeking the bits he liked. Well, she didn't have to worry about that. He was notorious for dating specifically Scandinavian blondes, with mile-high legs and breasts that, thanks to plastic surgery, sat up and saluted. Her curves were of the ordinary woman variety, round and placed exactly where nature intended them. It was her night gear that had made him take a second look.

Forced to dress conservatively during the day, she indulged herself in beautiful lingerie underneath. And a little ultra-feminine part of her psyche was ever such a tiny bit pleased that she'd wowed him. But she stuffed that thought away, along with those other pesky fantasies about him scooping her into his arms and carrying her upstairs to have his way with her.

Surreptitiously she lifted one hand to brush away any Danish crumbs that lingered on her lips. His eyes grew even more heavy lidded and Rose swallowed—hard.

'The result of your scurrilous accusation is I was escorted out of the hotel. It was very embarrassing…' She trailed off, realising he wouldn't be particularly interested in her feelings.

'I'm sure you'll recover.'

'I don't know why you're so sure. You don't know me. I could be very sensitive.'

He gave her an arrested look and for a spinning moment

it occurred to Rose that he might think she was referring to something else. More personal.

'No doubt,' he drawled, and she could feel the hot colour sweeping up her chest like a tide. 'But not on this subject. After all, you *were* trawling the boys this afternoon. Not the actions of a shrinking violet, *detka*.'

Rose's mouth fell open. 'I was *what*?'

'Trawling. Throwing out a net behind a boat and seeing what you can drag in.'

'I know what trawling is, and it has insulting connotations.'

'*Da*, but it is accurate.'

His expression was stone-cold accusation, and Rose's hard-won confidence took a tumble. She gathered her manners around her like defences. 'Did your mama raise you to talk to ladies with that mouth?' she demanded, trying not to let him see how upset she was.

Plato had the searing thought that his mother had been too busy working herself into the ground and drinking herself to death to mind what her street-smart young son was getting up to, but he pushed that aside as he stared down Texas. He couldn't remember any woman in the past who'd pulled him up on his manners. Mostly they were too busy trying to hold his attention. Apart from her little show this afternoon, Tex hadn't done anything other than defend herself since he'd turned up at her door. She actually looked a little wounded, and he had the unlikely thought that he was going too hard on her.

Da—right. The woman who had sashayed around that room today with her little gold pen wasn't hiding her light under a bushel.

She probably had the hide of a rhinoceros, even if her skin did look translucent as glass. *Chert*, he could see the shadow of a pale blue vein running along her throat from here, and there would be more tributaries of fine blue veins at her ankles, her wrists, the inner curves of her body.

She was really quite delicately built—which got lost in the sumptuous scale of the rest of her, cloaked now from his view.

He checked the drift of his thoughts under that throw. He wasn't going there.

The Wolves players weren't going there either.

Why that should raise a low, primitive growl in his subconscious he wasn't going to investigate. He snapped himself brutally out of the reverie.

Being ejected from hotels was an occupational hazard for a woman like this. How old was she? Twenty-one? Twenty-two? The lifestyle wasn't showing on her yet…

'Aren't you a little bit old for groupie tactics?'

Rose stiffened. Old? *Old?* 'I'm twenty-six,' she retaliated, then cursed herself for handing out personal information. It made all of this far too intimate.

'*Da*—older than half the boys.'

Trying not to feel as if she was halfway to her pension, Rose responded frostily, 'It's the modern era. Age is irrelevant.'

'Keep telling yourself that, princess.'

Rose's mouth fell open, and if she hadn't been so precariously positioned, and intimidated because of it, she would have leapt up and slapped his no-good, smirking face. Who did he think he was, *insinuating* she wanted to sleep with his players?

'I don't want to sleep with them,' she burst out. 'I want to date them!' *No, that wasn't right.* 'I mean I—'

'Let's get this clear,' he interrupted coldly. 'You came to the Dorrington to *date* an entire ice hockey team?'

Rose gave him a withering look. 'Yes,' she said drolly. 'I want to date twelve elite athletes. It's a dream of mine.'

Something approaching a smile tugged on Plato Kuragin's firm mouth, and for a moment Rose forgot how he had barged into her home, refused to let her dress, making these ridiculous accusations…because he'd almost smiled at her and some of her defensiveness crumbled away.

For a moment she spun on the thought that she could actually have a little fun with this. She could handle this guy. He was just trying to intimidate her—and, okay, doing a pretty good job of it—but nobody bossed her around any more. A long time ago she'd dug herself a hole of her own making with a man, but she'd got herself out of that. She was in charge of her life now. And maybe it wasn't such a bad thing to be seen as a *femme fatale*, capable of leading young men astray. Plato Kuragin was certainly making her think it was possible...

Rose shook her head. She couldn't believe she was even thinking that. She was letting the situation get to her. Letting his almost-smile get to her. She wasn't capable of leading *herself* astray, let alone twelve grown men! Yes, she'd acted recklessly, she knew that, and she hadn't bargained on the result she'd got. But now she was determined to handle it.

'I run a dating agency,' she explained crossly. 'I wanted to find dates for them.'

For a moment Plato Kuragin just stared. Stared until Rose felt the colour burning in her cheeks.

Stared until she felt forced to blurt out, 'Why are you staring at me like that?'

'The boys don't need help with that, *detka*.'

Rose rolled her eyes. 'I realise that. I was looking for publicity—'

His expression cooled, and his mouth formed a straight, hard line. 'Of course you were.'

'Don't make it sound like that!' she defended herself. 'You can't just come in here, insinuating horrid things about me. You don't know me! You invited yourself into my house, you won't let me get dressed—' She broke off as her voice tremored under the strain of keeping it all together.

Something flickered in his eyes, and his mouth softened as if he was going to say something.

'I'd really like to have my dinner and then go to bed...' she floundered.

For a moment his heavy gaze dropped to her mouth, and Rose had a startling and not completely unwelcome image of Plato Kuragin in that bed along with her.

She firmed her mouth.

'I don't know—perhaps this is how you do things in your

country. My knowledge of Russia is limited to *Dr Zhivago*. But in Canada men don't burst into the homes of women they don't know.'

'And you're keen to broaden that experience with my boys?' he inserted coolly.

'I know you're implying distasteful things, but that aside they are hardly boys. They're men, and they can make their own decisions.'

'Not whilst they're under contract, *detka*.'

That was that, then. That little dream was over. Rose took a breath and swallowed her disappointment. But she'd given it a go, she told herself, and that was huge for her. Maybe it had been a mistake but, *shoot*! If she was going to make them, they'd be *her* mistakes. This was the life she was meant to lead. Not one controlled by other people.

She guessed she had a passionate nature, and from all she'd heard that was a trait she'd inherited from her mother. Well, she was going to trust herself, her instincts and her passion from now on. Even if it got her into trouble.

She thought of Bill Hilliger, her ex-fiancé back in Houston, and how powerless she had felt to change anything at all during the four years they were together. Well, she'd darn well changed everything for herself now, and she hoped her mama would be proud of her determination and understand her need to leave behind the protection of her father and brothers. She *had* to make her own life, and she'd come all the way to Canada to do it—and if that meant dealing with the Plato Kuragins of this world, so be it.

It didn't hurt to pull her punches with him either. She had lied about her knowledge of Russia; she had taken six months of studying the language at college. Which was why she knew Plato Kuragin was calling her baby. *Baby*. As in *you're just a girl and I'm in charge*. He was such a jock. She hated jocks. She liked men with real jobs—hard-working men like her dad and her brothers. Men who removed their metaphorical hats when they spoke to a lady they had just been introduced to.

Men who wouldn't dream of just dropping in on a woman alone in the evening without an invitation.

This man, with his billions and blondes on tap and his jet-set lifestyle, clearly didn't have a clue how to treat a nice girl. Except he didn't see *her* as a nice girl, did he? He saw her as some sort of predacious tramp, leading his wet-behind-the-ears athletes astray.

And suddenly it wasn't so funny any more. She didn't want to be treated like something the cat had dragged in.

Not by this man.

The doorbell pealed.

Plato was on his feet. 'You will stay there,' he said repressively.

Oh, for goodness' sakes—she could answer her own door! However, Rose saw the advantage, and the moment he was gone she scrambled for the hall. Plato was dealing with the pizza delivery as she bolted up the stairs. She threw open her wardrobe doors and scouted for something nice. She didn't question why she wasn't pulling on yoga pants and a sweatshirt. She just knew no woman in her right mind would parade before Plato Kuragin in cheap cotton and fleece.

She grabbed a blue and white spotted silk and cotton dress off its hanger and made short work of exchanging throw and negligee for the flattering shoulder-to-ankle cut of the dress. It hinted at her curves but didn't make a show of them. She added a little yellow cardigan to cover her shoulders and arms, slicked some cherry-red colour over her lips and ran a brush through her hair. That would have to do. If she blowdried her curls straight it would just look as if she was trying.

She didn't want *trying*. She wanted everyday girl. A girl who didn't 'trawl' athletes or warrant unpleasant commentary on her actions.

Taking a deep breath, she came down the stairs, telling herself it was reasonable to change out of her nightwear when she had a guest—a *male* guest—and that he wouldn't read anything into that. And all women touched up their lipstick.

Perhaps the squirt of her favourite perfume hadn't been such a good idea.

Plato was in her kitchen. It was slightly disconcerting to find him there. He had her white flatware out on the bench and her fridge door open.

'You don't have beer, do you?' he asked, crouching down to get a look inside.

Rose told herself not to stare at that very taut behind clad in brutally faithful tailored trousers. Then she tried to work out why she wasn't objecting to him making himself so comfortable in her home.

'There's just an open bottle of wine,' she heard herself say faintly, 'or a soft drink.'

Her kitchen was so tiny two people were a crowd, and when one of those people was a six-foot-six-inch male with a breadth across his shoulders that made Rose feel slight in comparison there really wasn't anywhere to go. Rose backed up as far as she could into the kitchen cupboard, and jammed its handle into the curve of her bottom.

'Glasses?' He straightened up, looked over his shoulder at her.

Rose stilled as he turned, those rainy-night eyes taking her in as if she were an oasis in the desert. She waited for him to say something. Although what he'd say she didn't know. Something along the lines of, *You've changed,* which was obvious, but somehow she didn't think that was what he was thinking.

Except he couldn't be thinking what she *thought* he was thinking.

Because why would a man get overheated about a dress when he'd already seen her in her hot-to-trot underthings?

Men looked at her. She couldn't walk down a city street without second glances, a wolf whistle, something that cheered up her day. But she well knew the pitfalls of being judged on her bra size, and she dressed to diminish rather than play up any sex appeal she might possess. Men appreciated aspects of her body, but none of that had prepared her for how Plato Kuragin was looking at her now, or the effect it was having on her.

'In the cupboard just above—next to your head.' He was so tall nothing was actually above him.

He stared back at her blankly.

Oh, my Lord, this is so silly. 'I'll get them,' she said, a little embarrassed, and crossed to him, reaching up to open the cupboard door.

He barely shifted, just looked down at her, ever so slightly poleaxed. 'I was told you run a dating agency,' he said in a rough voice. 'Is that true?'

'Uh-huh. Date with Destiny.' For some reason this less-than-sure-of-himself Plato Kuragin was letting the real Rose uncurl herself from hibernation for the first time since he'd arrived. She even angled up her chin and gave him a curious look, which was a mistake because they were awfully close all of a sudden.

She brought down her arms with the glasses in her hand and her right breast brushed very definitely against his arm. She felt his bicep contract and saw his eyes go hard and hot as they dipped lower. Her nipples came out to play, and suddenly her brains just scrambled.

She turned to set the glasses down with a clatter and put some physical distance between them. The bench. *There.* No one could get through wood and Formica—although looking at the heavy musculature in those arms she wouldn't bet money on it. *Stop staring at his arms, Rose.* What on earth was wrong with her?

'I was at the Dorrington Hotel drumming up business, if you really want to know,' she said a tad awkwardly, because suddenly it really mattered that he thought well of her. 'And that's the total extent of this agenda you say I have.'

'Drumming up business?' he repeated, but Rose got the impression she could have said anything.

He was intent on appreciating the look of her—her hair, her

face, the cling of the dress down her legs. Was it her imagination or did he literally rip his gaze away from her as he held up the wine to check its label?

Rose stifled a groan, her attention shifting to how down-market all this must seem to him. The house, the wine, her... 'It's just a regular white from the supermarket,' she explained, her voice tailing off. It was an echo from her other life—the one in Houston where she'd never been quite good enough for Bill and his hoity-toity family—and that it should assail her here and now dumped a bucket on her fantasy.

Dammit, if she wanted a fantasy she could have it! She wanted to enjoy Plato Kuragin whilst he was here, because goodness knew he could vanish as abruptly as he had arrived.

Plato reached into his pocket and whipped out a cell phone. She watched as he thumbed the keypad.

'What are you doing?'

'Sorting out food. We can do better than pizza and cheap wine, *detka*.'

'You're ordering a meal? For both of us?'

'*Da*, is there a problem?'

He'd had her thrown out of the Dorrington, invaded her home, virtually forced her to sit in front of him in her under-wear, threatened her with legal action...and now he wanted to share a meal with her! *Was there a problem?*

'I guess that would be all right,' she murmured, looking down at her bare feet, tracing circles with her red-painted big toenail on the tiled floor.

You could *almost* call this a date, a little voice whispered in her ear.

Stop it, Rose.

'We will sit in a restaurant and relax and talk,' said Plato, rounding the bench.

Rose told herself to hold her ground, play it cool. She wasn't going to hop about like a frightened rabbit. Truth be told, this was so much more than she had hoped for when she'd crashed the Dorrington press conference this afternoon.

He closed a big hand over her wool-clad shoulder and for a moment the gesture lingered, as if he was learning the delicacy of her bone structure, the roundness that was so much a part of her, as if his touch was about to turn into something else. He turned her effortlessly towards the door.

He wasn't really asking, but he didn't strike Rose as the kind of guy who asked. He seemed just to issue directives and take what he wanted—and why that should send happy messages to her lace-clad regions she wasn't going to second-guess or question. Besides, this wasn't about him controlling her, because this was what she wanted.

'We're going out?' she asked redundantly.

'*Da*, is that a problem?'

'I guess not,' she prevaricated.

'You can tell me about this business of yours,' he said, in that growly, sexy Russian voice of his.

Rose glowed.

I will. And whilst you're being all he-man and Russian I'll convince you that being my Date with Destiny is the least you can do, seeing as you burst in here and scared me out of my wits, you big lug.

'I guess that would be okay,' she responded with a little smile.

Being foreign, Plato Kuragin obviously didn't understand that if you gave a Texan woman an inch she'd take a mile.

Yes, this was definitely a date.

CHAPTER FOUR

THE night was finally making sense.

He'd laid eyes on her—what?—four hours ago? Now he had her in his car. He was taking her to dinner. He would possibly be introducing himself to the delights of her body in a few more hours.

Everything that had seemed murky, uncertain, almost out of character, suddenly fitted. A beautiful woman with an agenda… He'd had her investigated, he'd narrowed down and dismissed the problem, and now he could move in to enjoy what was on offer.

And she had a lot to offer.

But she was peering at him as if he might vanish at any moment. He wanted to tell her she had nothing to fear on that score. He was hers until he sent her home in a cab tomorrow morning.

The thought brought his attention to those small hands curled together in her lap. Uneasily he took in the modest, classic cut of her dress. The only concessions she had made to highlighting her appearance were dangling earrings and a midnight-blue bolero jacket she'd replaced the cardigan with. Little details, but they were cutting through his hard-won cynicism like a scythe.

There would always be women of a certain type hanging around elite sports teams. He didn't take advantage of it. That wasn't why he'd bought the club. That had been personal. A way to hold on to his roots.

He wasn't interested in a woman who had so little self-respect she would throw herself at a man simply because he had some fame and she wanted publicity.

Rose wasn't one of those women.

Sure, she was after a little star athlete for her hobby/business/whatever, but she wasn't selling herself. When he'd looked up and seen her standing there in a long dress, her hair tidied, her lips gleaming, she'd knocked his half-arsed suspicions sideways. Rose had gone to some trouble with her appearance—the sort of trouble that told him she was embarrassed about being found in her satiny nothings and was trying to remedy the impression. She also clearly had no idea how incredibly sexy she was, or she wouldn't have put on that romantic dress.

Women usually took more clothes off when they were trying to play up their sex appeal. Somehow with Rose the inverse was true—or maybe it was something to do with how he was responding to her?

He'd used to dream of dating girls like this once upon a time, back in the Urals mining town he'd grown up in. Even then he'd come with a warning sign—not the sort of boy any of the neighbourhood parents had wanted their daughters bringing home.

Something stirred uneasily in the back of his mind. Rose smiled across at him. A nice middle-class girl going out to dinner. With him.

Someone really needed to warn her.

Maybe not a cab. Definitely not a cab. He'd drive her home himself.

Da, that was sorted. He waited for some of the tension he was holding in his shoulders to trickle away. It remained stubbornly where it was.

Unaccustomed to scruples when it came to hooking up with women looking to profit by their association, he applied his mind to something that wasn't soft and warm and playing footsie with his conscience—tomorrow's schedule. At 5:00 a.m.

he had a conference call from south-east Asia that would take him through to seven. Then a breakfast dialogue with Canadian NHL representatives. Then he had to deal with the legal issues surrounding the Sazanov brothers being arrested for drug possession—huge red tape there. He had a lunch with investors from the Arab Emirates, who were flying up from Washington for the privilege, and a meet-and-greet with local mayoral officials, and then the Wolves' last practice match before they took on Canada's finest on Friday night.

But right now, strapped into his borrowed baby, the very nice Ferrari, was his reward for taking a little trouble tonight and dealing with one of the finer points of the tour personally.

He'd wine and dine her, and plunder her incredible treasure chest, and give her what she wanted in the morning: a little access to the players.

Da, baby, he thought as she peeked one of those curious glances at him, *play your cards right and I'm all your Prince Charmings come at once.*

Rose had never ridden in a sports car. They were certainly different. She felt as if she was very close to the road but at the same time gliding at speed over water because the ride was so smooth. Plato was doing that guy thing of making everything he did with the gears look effortless, but he was clearly doing it to impress her.

She could have told him just turning up had impressed her. She wasn't going to forget having six feet six inches of gorgeous Russian male in her kitchen in a hurry.

She hadn't liked his pushing his way into her house, or refusing to let her go and change out of her underthings, or the way he'd made all sorts of lewd accusations about her motives. Although, actually, that had given her a bit of a thrill. She thought she'd left confident, take-charge men behind in Texas. Apparently they bred them in Russia too.

She'd missed it, and she'd missed this part of herself. It had been a long time since a man had challenged her. After her four years in Houston she was super-sensitive to any man trying to get his way with her, but she just didn't get that vibe from Plato. He was so incredibly confident she got the impression he assumed the world would bend his way—and it probably did.

Besides, it was past time to trust her instincts, and she told herself she could turn tail at any time. Not that this was going anywhere. A guy who looked like this, with money and power and prestige, didn't date girls like her. He handed them his coat or a tip.

He didn't wrap them up in their coat, keep an arm around them as he escorted them outside, and put them in a luxury car as if they belonged there, his big body radiating heat and security and protection.

Rose repressed a little sigh. She wouldn't be confusing to-night's little fantasy with anything more meaningful. Plato Kuragin was hardly going to hole up in Toronto and date her! Besides, she was here for the business. She had some funds to raise and this guy was big in funds. She could take a little jump into the unknown, enjoy herself for a while, but the bigger picture was the business.

Good to get that straight.

Twenty minutes later, as he seated her at their table, she was still thinking business even as her inner princess did a pirou-ette. The restaurant was on the seventy-fifth floor of a famous building. Rose had read about it in a glossy magazine recently. She just hadn't expected she'd ever be dining here.

'You could have just asked, you know,' she said with a lit-tle smile.

'Asked?' Plato took his seat opposite her and leaned in closer, his focus intent on her face as if she fascinated him.

'To have dinner with me.'

'Is that what this is about?' he asked.

'What else could it be?'

He was silent for a moment. 'I apologise for making as-sumptions,' he said, in that deep, dark voice.

'I hadn't realised you'd made any.' But they both knew he

had. 'Oh, you mean the groupie comment? Sorry to disappoint you. I'm about as interested in sport as you are in lipstick.'

'I don't know about that,' he replied, his voice pitched low and intimate.

He eased forward, bringing his forearms down on the table, and suddenly it felt awfully small and insubstantial between them—although if she looked around the restaurant their table was no smaller than anyone else's.

'I could develop a fascination for the subject.'

It was a clichéd line and they both knew it. Plato didn't back off, though. If anything the space between them seemed to get smaller and smaller, until all she could see was the suggestion of what his firm mouth could do to her lipstick and the gleam of purpose behind those rain-dark eyes.

Rose knew it was her birthright as a Southern woman to flirt, but this man was outside her experience—and she also wasn't sure if overt flirting was going to get her what she wanted. Although at this point she wasn't entirely certain what that was.

Plato leaned back and gave the *maître d'* instructions about their meals, but his eyes never left hers. Rose was glad of the low lights in the restaurant, the candles between them, the shadows that hopefully went some way to disguising how susceptible she was to him.

'You wanted to hear about my business?'

'*Da*, the destiny date,' he said easily.

Rose couldn't repress a smile at the way he said it in that deep, dark voice. As if it were a little children's toy she was wheeling out when of course it was so much more.

'I'm looking to sign one or two of your players up to do a publicity piece for my agency.'

'You didn't think to approach our PR people?'

'Uh-huh, I'm sure *that* would have worked.'

He lifted those big shoulders in a heavy shrug that said, *What can I do? I'm an important man. I don't handle the small stuff.*

Yet he had. He'd turned up at her front door.

'Why did you turn up at my house?'

Yes, why not just blurt it out, Rose?

He seemed about to say something, then shook his head as if whatever he had been thinking had amused him. 'My security team showed me your blog,' he said.

Rose scrambled to remember what she had written.

'I was concerned, naturally. I thought I would check it out.'

The blog or her? Rose peered back at him warily.

'Why would you be concerned? I didn't defame anybody. It was just a silly laugh.'

'Is that what it was, Rose?' He didn't show it by any particular movement in his face or note in his voice but Rose sensed his sudden watchfulness.

'My blog bothered you,' she said slowly.

'Let's just say it drew attention to a couple of things the media don't need to get wind of. But I accept you are who you appear to be, Rose. A young woman running an internet dating site.'

'Is this about the Sazanov brothers?'

He shrugged negligently. 'It doesn't matter now. It's taken care of.'

'Then why did you come to my house?'

Plato drummed the table with his left hand. 'Sometimes even grown men can behave like hormonal boys, *dushka*.'

Rose forgot about the Sazanov brothers. Forgot about the embarrassment of him reading her silly blog. She even—almost—forgot about how he had bossed her around in her own home, in her underwear. Was he saying he was attracted to her? He'd wanted to see her again?

'You wanted to see me,' she said, hoping the thrill that gave her didn't show—or her subsequent embarrassment.

'Da.' He didn't look embarrassed at all. 'I meet beautiful women all the time. Many give me their contact details. You did so in an unusual way.'

Rose's excitement dimmed. So much for being special.

'Then, of course, I learned you had done the same with each and every member of the team. I was—disappointed.'

'Right.' She struggled to find something amusing to quip back at him, but she was feeling her own disappointment.

'I was concerned as to your motives, and when Security located you I decided to handle it myself.' A half-smile tugged at that firm mouth of his. 'As I said, my judgement was somewhat clouded by other considerations. The main one being I wanted to see you again.'

Rose gripped her champagne flute. 'Well, there is that,' she said faintly.

'It's fortunate I did,' he said. 'I wouldn't have liked a member of my security team coming to your door tonight, finding you in that—what do you call it?'

Rose's mouth felt dry and her head a little light.

'Nightie,' she said airlessly.

'You wear that to bed? Alone?'

Someone had turned up the temperature in the room. Rose jerked her glass to her lips. 'Mmm…' She fudged her answer and swallowed.

'Such a waste.' He was watching her with obvious interest, his eyes dark and moving over her flushed face.

Rose almost dropped her glass. Liquid splashed. She looked about for a cloth but Plato was already reaching across, blotting the tablecloth, his eyes never leaving hers.

'I didn't ask you,' he said, in that deep accented voice that thrilled her to her toes. 'Are you unattached? Is there someone?'

For almost two years she had been the most unattached woman in Toronto, and right up until this very moment she had been happy to keep it that way. 'No, there's no one.' Why was her voice all breathless and girly? It made her sound like such a push-over.

For this man I could very well be a pushover.

'I celebrate that news,' he said with a slight smile.

He was so *foreign*. So dangerous to her equilibrium. One

moment they were having a business dinner, and suddenly it was all sex. Yes, it was definitely about sex.

She told herself she hoped she wasn't such a ninny that she was going to fall for all that macho bunkum about her nightie and being alone in her bed and needing a man…

But she was very much afraid she was.

Oh, for land sakes pull yourself together, Rose.

'The reason you're here isn't because I wrote my cell number on your hand,' she said defensively. 'You got ticked off because I did the same for each and every one of your precious players.'

He chuckled, and the sound was a lovely rumble in his chest that had Rose tilting forward to be closer to it. Self-preservation should have seen her putting some space between them, because right about now she was becoming aware she felt a little out of control with this man. It was as if she kept slip-sliding towards him, and she didn't really understand why this was so.

'I'm here for the same reason why every one of those players was given strict instructions *not* to use that number,' he replied easily. 'You're an incredibly beautiful woman.'

She was? Rose struggled to find something to answer that, but her mind was spinning like a wheel without grip on *incredibly beautiful*. Trying to focus, she felt her brain slowly start to function again, and she… Hang on, what did he mean the players had been instructed not to use her number?

'You use your femininity to your advantage,' he observed lazily, as if this pleased him. His lashes were at half-mast. Everything about him reeked sexual confidence. 'I'm not complaining.'

Pushing through the dozens of messages the woman in her was reacting to, as if sexual switches were being thrown here, there and everywhere, Rose grasped onto the one thing she knew was true. She most certainly did *not* play the womanly wiles card! And if the players couldn't use her number this afternoon had been a waste of time. She was back at square one.

'You told the players not to call me?'

He shrugged. 'This cannot come as a surprise, Rose.'

Yes, it did. It *did* come as a surprise. 'Then what's this supposed to be? Why did you bring me here?'

'I came to your house tonight to warn you off.' He spoke as if she were making him repeat the obvious. 'When I discovered you were not what I imagined you to be I reconsidered my options. I chose not to waste the evening.'

Rose made a little sound—half-laugh, half-groan.

'Rose?' The coolness was gone. Plato sat forward slightly.

Rose couldn't believe how stupid she'd been. It was as though she'd been playing a game, and in truth she had been—enjoying the ride, allowing her fantasies and her passionate nature to carry her along for once and not putting on the brakes. But here it was, cold, hard reality, and none of it was helping her business.

Familiar sensations of being overwhelmed flooded through her, shifting the new pylons of hope she'd built, reminding her all too clearly of her recent past in Houston when her every decision had been countermanded.

'I have to get out of here,' she said, not even realising she'd spoken aloud until she saw him shift in his chair. Rocketing to her feet, Rose reached for her clutch purse. 'I'm sure you've had an interesting time tonight, Mr Kuragin, but I have to get up in the morning and try to find a way to salvage the advertising spot I bought for Date with Destiny. So if you'll excuse me, it's been…' she struggled for a word '…different.'

'Sit down, Rose,' he said, half out of his seat.

'Go to hell, Plato,' she replied, tossing her hair over her shoulder as she stalked out.

CHAPTER FIVE

PLATO was not a man who indulged in introspection, but even so he acknowledged that the last ten minutes had not gone well as he strode after the retreating back of a very angry skirt-twitching, heels-flashing Texan woman.

He had already pinpointed his mistake. As soon as he'd had Rose buckled up in the Ferrari he should have taken her directly to his hotel suite—possibly cuffed those delicate little wrists of hers and turned all that spitting and scratching to happy sighs of pleasure. She was definitely a woman who needed a strong hand because she had demonstrated she didn't take well to direction. Clearly giving Rose options was where the trouble had started.

She had just exercised one.

Which required him to chase her. He didn't mind the exercise, but he was troubled by the suspicion that one night with Rose wasn't going to be enough. *Troubled* probably wasn't the right word. *Challenged* sprang to mind.

Who knew Texas had a temper on her?

Rose stomped out of the restaurant and was halted by the bank of lifts. Damn the seventy-fifth floor. She should have insisted on a walk-in diner where the getting out was good. She didn't belong in places like this—all silver service and postage-stamp food, and wait staff who made more money than she did.

Folding her arms, tapping her foot, Rose watched the numbers light up. She could barely hold still. She wanted to hit something.

She'd changed her mind about Plato Kuragin. He was definitely too much for her to handle. Besides, she'd had her fill of arrogant take-charge men. Plato Kuragin was just an *über*-example of the breed. In fact she could actually *see* him sitting around the Three Rings Bar in her hometown, Fidelity Falls, with her brothers, taking up a ridiculous amount of room with their legs and shoulders and egos, drinking beer and bourbon and talking about women as if they were cattle—each girl a little steer who needed the right amount of rope and a little rough handling to let her know who was boss.

Tonight she'd had all the rough handling she was going to put up with in this lifetime. This was Toronto, for land sakes! There were all sorts of laws protecting women from take-charge men—one of them being the trusty restraining order.

The doors in front of her opened and she threw herself inside, feeling absurdly disappointed. It wasn't that she'd expected him to follow her. She'd taken his number. He knew he wasn't getting laid this side of Christmas when it came to *this* little patooty.

A large male hand reached across hers and pushed the ground floor button.

'Oh, no, you don't, buster!'

She moved to step out, but he literally blocked her with his body. His far too big, muscular male body, that towered over her even in her favourite heels. She was nose to pectoral with his hard, wide chest. She knew another woman might have felt overwhelmed by his size, his intent, even a little threatened. But she wasn't some city-bred miss who thought milk came from cartons. No, sirree. She'd ridden her first bull when she was eleven. She could take on shoulders and spurs with one hand tied behind her back.

She poked him—hard—in the centre of his chest for emphasis. 'There's only room for one person in this lift, cowboy, and it ain't you.'

'Is that right?' he growled.

She hadn't expected him to come back hard—but then she hadn't really thought he would follow her...had she?

The doors closed and she was trapped in there with him. The lift began to descend.

She wouldn't be giving him the pleasure. Rose stepped back, plastered her clutch bag to her waist, and stared dead straight ahead as if he didn't exist. Her foot began to tap. She really couldn't help it. Her body felt like the energy map of southwest Canada.

He was looking her up and down as if she was a calf he was thinking of buying.

'If this is foreplay, *detka*, I'm looking forward to the main event.'

Rose's foot stopped tapping. Her head swivelled. '*What* did you say to me?'

'Usually dinner and some conversation appeals to the civilised man in me, but if you need drama to get in the mood we can go there.'

'The only place we're going is down,' she bit back—then could have kicked herself. She half expected him to say something disgusting, because men always did—twisting a girl's words, making her say the things they wanted to hear.

Except Plato did none of those things. Instead he laughed softly, and the sound was so blatantly sexual that Rose felt the backs of her knees go. *Shoot!* She was in some trouble with this man. He had all the cool, calm and control and she had the blasted trembles.

Against her better judgement Rose risked another glance at him. She wanted to shake him and demand to know why he wouldn't help her out. She wasn't asking for all that much— just a couple of his players for an hour of their time. She was going to pay them.

Pay them, Rose? A smidgeon of what they're worth?

No, to be truthful she was hoping they would overlook the

modicum of money she was offering and do it because it was fun. She would bat her eyes at them and…

Drat this man for making her feel as if she was selling something besides her business.

'You've got some nerve, you know,' she erupted. 'Dragging me out here, making with the "tell me about your business, baby" and then thinking insincere flattery is going to get you laid. If we were in Texas my daddy would take a bullwhip to you.'

'Fortunate we're not in Texas, then,' he responded as the lift gave a slight movement and the doors began to open. 'Although I'm beginning to understand why you like it rough, *dushka*.'

Rose didn't think, she just reacted, slamming her purse hard into his mid-section. 'There you go—rough enough for you?'

Infuriatingly he didn't flinch. But she moved, striking out for the foyer, aware she was only a hair's breadth from losing it altogether. The intimate things he had said to her, asking her if she was single, making her think if only for a moment that he was interested…

It hurt. She didn't know why, but for a little while there she'd let down her guard a little, believed him…

Yes, he was interested. And she knew *exactly* what he was interested in.

Making a fool of her.

Been there, done that. She wasn't hanging around for another round of humiliation. She should have known this wasn't going to turn into a fairy tale. Hell, she'd known that in her head from the get-go. It was just that when he'd looked at her in the kitchen with that slightly keel-hauled expression, and put her into the car as if she was made of precious porcelain, she'd started to get ideas…

Stupid ideas. She knew darn well through experience that fairy tales were just that. Four years engaged to a man who undermined her at every turn had shown her just how dangerous believing in a man could be. No, you needed to take a good, long, hard *cool* look at a man and not expect him to be Prince

Charming. She made a living telling people to use their heads before their hearts in choosing a mate—she had boxes on a form to fill out, for land sakes—and there she was, making eyes over a restaurant table with a man who would be gone in a couple of days, back to the land of the rich and famous.

She looked around desperately for the exit, wondering what would happen now, if he would follow her or leave her to it. Whilst her head was telling her to find the nearest cab and jump in, she was literally humming with energy and she didn't know what to do with it. She would have liked to have thrown a punch, busted him one right on his annoyingly straight nose, but they weren't in Texas and it probably didn't go down so well here. And it would ruin that ladylike image she was supposed to be toting.

Not that *he* thought she was ladylike. He seemed to think she was some sort of take-what-she-could-get grifter...

Who was now standing on the pavement looking around for a cab rank that didn't exist.

Plato nodded to the busboy, who leapt out of his Ferrari with the wistful expression of someone who'd been given the keys to his lifelong dream for a moment and now had to give them back.

'Hold it a minute, will you, kid?'

He walked slowly but deliberately across the paved plaza towards the woman pacing up and down, craning her neck as she watched the traffic.

In her blue wool coat with the collar turned up against the cold Rose appeared every bit as ladylike as she had when he'd looked up and found her standing in her little kitchen, with that dazed and uncertain expression on her lovely face as if finding men rummaging through her refrigerator wasn't something that happened to her every day.

It had touched something very basic inside him—a chivalrous urge to explain himself to her, to reassure her he was a good guy. To get her to smile at him.

And right now in front of him was an unhappy girl who

looked cold and defenceless on a city street—and *he* had brought her here, he was responsible for her. *Chert.*

'Rose, you will get in the car. I will take you home.'

She ignored him. If a woman could hold herself any stiffer she would break.

'You will not get a cab.' She liked it when he told her what to do. He'd figured that one out. 'Do not make me carry you.'

She wheeled around, hands on hips. 'What's that supposed to mean?'

'Sto?'

She didn't look cold and defenceless. She looked as if she was on fire.

'Are you making a crack about my weight?'

Plato just stared at her. She was so beautiful, and she was so angry, and he had no idea what she was talking about. It could have been the language barrier, or the fact she was a woman and they rarely made logical sense, but right then all he wanted to do was…

This.

He closed the distance between them and roped his arm around her waist. He moved too quickly for her to resist and propelled her a few steps to the wall of the building, pinning her right up against him, feet dangling in those silly little blue heels of hers, nose to nose, breathing hard.

He smiled at her stunned expression. 'Are you listening to me now, Rose?'

She blinked. She wasn't struggling. That was good.

Very slowly he let her slide down his body to her feet. She stood there, trembling a little, looking up at him. Exactly where he wanted her.

He leaned in, bracketing the wall either side of her with his arms. He carefully cupped one side of her face with his big hand. 'I had no idea why I'd driven across town to your house tonight until you opened that door—are we clear?'

Rose blinked.

'But this has nothing to do with you being tricked out in

sexy lingerie, or using my players as sexual leverage with you. Does that clear things up?'

No, it didn't clear anything up. But she was really hoping the wall behind her didn't collapse, because it was all that was holding her up at this point. She had thought she knew what sexual excitement was, but it turned out that until this moment she hadn't had a clue.

His gaze roamed over her face.

'You are so very beautiful.' He feathered her dark eyebrow with his thumb. 'But until now I had no idea how incredibly arousing a woman who doesn't pluck her eyebrows can be.' His thumb moved down to stroke the fullness of her cheek. 'Or how soft her skin is when she doesn't cake it in make-up, or how tempting her lips are when they're soft and unpainted.' His thumb came to rest on her full lower lip.

For a throbbing moment Rose considered telling him she *did* actually pluck the odd stray hair from her eyebrows, and she *was* wearing a little powder, and her lips were courtesy of a very famous French fragrance house—but, really, how many secrets should a girl give away?

Instead she obeyed an instinct as old as time and opened her mouth ever so slightly. She bit down gently on that thumb pressing so sweetly onto her lower lip, drawing him into her mouth just for a moment, using her tongue.

She knew the instant she had him. His features were pulled taut and extraordinarily Slavic because of it, and his dark eyes went the colour of the ocean ten thousand metres deep. She knew, sure as sugar, that famously incisive brain of his had just moved below his belt.

She bit down hard and he whipped his hand away from her, swearing softly in Russian. Plato examined the reddened blunt tip of his thumb, bearing her toothmarks, his expression unreadable.

Maybe that had been a bad idea, Rose thought as female instinct shouted, *Back up*. But the new and improved, speak-your-mind-and-assert-yourself Rose knew she had to hold her ground. She forced out the words she needed to have him hear. 'That's as close as you're coming to heaven with me, Mr Billionaire. Remember that when you're lying in that cold bed of yours tonight. Does that clear things up?'

He gave her such a long, silent look that she lost a bit of ground, and then he brought one of those big hands up to cradle her head and gently rubbed the back of her neck, as if she were a kid in need of soothing.

'I had no idea you were hiding this much temperament under all that luminous classic beauty.' He chuckled. 'Do you know? I'm almost tempted to give you what you want because in the end it's not such a big deal for me. But I find I'm enjoying the fireworks too much to give in just yet.'

Rose hissed an indrawn breath and gave his chest an almighty shove. Again he barely shifted.

'Get off me, you big lug.'

He released her slowly, the eyes he settled on her not giving much away. But she fancied she could see something in them she'd not seen before. Respect.

But respect wasn't permission to utilise his athletes.

'You will let me drive you home, Rose,' he stated, as if she had no say in it.

But she did. She knew she could refuse. She also knew Plato Kuragin could behave decently when he wanted to. Which made it all worse.

She shrugged, as if it didn't matter either way, and walked away from him, back towards the building entrance. But it did matter.

She nudged up the collar on her coat—not only to shield her face from the wind but to hide it from his incisive view. He was playing games with her and it was pushing her buttons. Whatever he said, she wasn't going to stick out her chest and bat her eyes to get what she wanted. Sure, she'd used a little charm to get her number into those boys' hands, but she hadn't been that overt. It had been innocent and hopeful, that was all.

Plato Kuragin could drive her home if that made him feel better, but he knew what he'd done to her, and she knew after tonight she would never see him again.

CHAPTER SIX

PLATO stood in the owners' box, arms folded, watching the running play as commentary from the scorekeepers' bench was pumped into the earpiece he was wearing. It was a practice match, but it was their last before the game on Friday night. On Saturday the team would be flying on to Montreal, and he would be headed east to Moscow.

He harboured no strong feelings of roots in the Russian capital, but he had an apartment there and it would be good to sink out of the public eye for a few days whilst he went through a round of meetings with the new board. He'd lined up some female company, but last night, when that particular woman's name had flashed up on his cell, he hadn't picked up—even though he had already driven Rose home.

His mind had been otherwise occupied.

Seeing Rose to her door and having that door soundly slammed in his face had been a novel experience. Watching her light go on upstairs, standing across the road, leaning against the Ferrari, had been another. He hadn't realised he was doing it until a late-night jogger idled on the pavement behind him and asked what he was doing. Plato could have asked himself the same question—and what the hell was it with that neighbourhood? Why were they all so vitally interested in Rose's well-being?

'Just seeing a lady home,' he said, thinking it was good to know she was safe in this street.

'Rose Harkness?' said the jogger. 'Nice girl.'

'So I've heard.'

As he'd got the hell out of the suburbs he'd been humming Ravel's *Boléro* under his breath.

If he'd been one of those New Age guys who thought their women were proto-men, who did not deserve to be looked after and protected and cosseted and humoured in their little idiosyncrasies, he might not have put in the effort he had that morning. But he understood factoring in Rose's little quirks was all part of the game, and it was going to take a little finessing on his part.

He'd had a face-to-face with a couple of the boys, Rykov and Lieven, and sent them Rose's way. He'd made sure twenty-four yellow roses were delivered to her home, and had lined up a stunning lakeview house, a chef, and himself as entertainment for this evening.

He could give her two nights, and he intended to make the most of them.

But he had yet to call her.

In the back of his mind he knew a phone call wasn't going to cut it with Rose. It would give her too much opportunity to cut and run. Better to let her day run its course. She would be happy because her little destiny date had been achieved. She would be whistling Dixie—wasn't that the expression?

Da, and then he would just turn up and take away her options. Give her new ones. And warm himself against all that stunning fire simmering in Rose's sumptuous body.

He ignored the voice in his head that told him to forget it, to walk away. The voice that told him his lifestyle and her girl-next-door vibe made this a collision course of disastrous proportions.

He'd grown up tough in that mining town in the Urals, the son of an unmarried mother who had turned up on her parents' doorstep after a year in Moscow pregnant and unable or unwilling to name the father. His grandmother had never let him forget how much he owed them, or how unwanted he was.

His mother had worked, drunk and succumbed to a diseased liver by the time he was fifteen. By then he'd been uncontrollable, a menace to lawful society, a boy nobody wanted. The only things he had been good at were using his body as the violent instrument it was, and his sharp mathematical mind to run scams.

Recognising his skill with a stick and a puck, and his take-no-prisoners attitude, the local ice hockey coach, Pavel Ignatieff, had stepped in and given his sixteen-year-old self the break his grandparents, fate and the town hadn't cut him. It had turned his life around. He'd been proving himself worth Ignatieff's while ever since.

His old coach would understand if not necessarily approve of the old-fashioned, let-me-at-her lust that was driving him after Rose. But in his experience the only way to get what you wanted was to take it and be damned, and that was overcoming any finer scruples he might have. Besides, Rose was a grown woman, and after her performance at the press conference and again last night he didn't doubt she knew the score.

Rose parked her blue jalopy under the stadium and made her way up to the private, ticket-holders-only entrance.

An old guy in a baseball cap was watching a black-and-white movie on a small set inside a glass office. Rose gave him her name—Sasha Rykov had said he'd leave it at the gate—and she was waved through.

If only the rest of this day would go so smoothly—but Rose was carrying an even bigger basket of butterflies in her belly than the one she'd toted at the press conference.

It could so utterly and disastrously backfire on her.

As it had last night when she'd lost her temper with Plato and gone in fists flailing.

She'd grown up in a family where pushing and shoving was an everyday occurrence. To get what she wanted she would pummel her brothers into submission, knowing they couldn't pummel back. If she shrieked loud enough they always gave in. Last night she had fallen back on those habits she'd learned in her girlhood.

Humiliatingly, she'd exposed that hurt, uncontrollable little girl to the man she had been trying to win over. And win him over she was definitely trying to do. *Because let's be honest, Rose,* the little voice of her conscience intervened, *the I'm-doing-it-for-the-business line just isn't cutting it any more.* The minute Plato Kuragin had told her he'd wanted to see her again it had gone out of the window.

In the brief time she'd known this man she had revealed more of her true nature than she had in the four years she'd spent as Bill Hilliger's fiancée. He brought it out in her—the earthy little country girl underneath a layering of urban poise. But Plato Kuragin wasn't the sort of man to be swayed by temper tantrums. No, he'd pretty much spelt it out to her what *he* wanted. If she used her *femininity to her advantage* she could just about get anything she wanted out of him. But what sort of woman did he think that made her?

She knew exactly what sort, and it made her angry all over again. She knew who those women were. You couldn't grow up in a household with four older brothers and miss the fact that the girls they had respect for were the ones who didn't play that card.

Well, she was done making a fool of herself. He was passing through Toronto. He would be gone in a few days. She had a business to run. Today was D-day.

She'd left her house at dawn this morning, after not much sleep, to salvage what she could of her advertising spot. At one o'clock a small film crew was turning up at a local restaurant and shooting would go ahead for Date with Destiny's ad spot on a popular morning show.

She'd be forced to go to Plan B and use a jobbing actor friend in lieu of a gorgeous athlete. It wouldn't have nearly the impact, but she hadn't any choice.

She had been about to make that call when a number had flashed up that she didn't recognise.

'Rose Harkness,' she'd said, endeavouring to sound cheerful. 'Rose?'

The voice had been Russian, and for a moment the breath had stopped in her throat. The moment had spun on…and then collapsed. Too light, too young, too…not Plato.

And the fact that it had mattered so much brought her right back into the moment. She *really* didn't want to think about Plato right now.

'Yes, it's Rose Harkness,' she had said, all business.

'*Zdrasvityze*, it's Sasha.'

Rose's brain had whirred into gear. Sasha Rykov. Star goalie for the Wolves. Clearly the blanket ban had holes in it, or someone hadn't paid much attention to the boss.

A little spark of hope had lit in her chest.

'Sasha, I'm so pleased to hear from you.'

'Can I be seeing you, Rose?' His voice had come youthful and confident and direct down the line.

Rose had lifted her gaze ceilingwards and mouthed a little prayer of gratitude.

'Oh, yes, Sasha, you can *definitely* be seeing me.'

She was back in the game.

So Rose had spent the afternoon at the restaurant with Sasha Rykov and one of her girlfriends—Phoebe—hovering as the couple enjoyed a nice lunch under the glare of cameras and a film crew. Sasha had flirted outrageously with Phoebe, and given them a couple of lines they'd be able to use in the promo.

After the shoot one of the television executives had rung with questions about the contract she'd handed them. Sasha's signature wasn't enough. According to their legal advisers the Wolves management would need to sign off on it, even though she had explained Sasha's fee would be going to a charity.

She had been faced with the reality that without Plato's consent the footage might never be aired. She would have to see him again, and it would be embarrassing—because she was all too aware that last night she hadn't behaved well. But neither had he, and her last memory of him was of his face as she'd slammed her door.

Maybe it wouldn't be so bad, she told herself. She was hoping Plato would see the humorous side. She was hoping he would shrug those big shoulders and say, *Da, baby, you make your play. Just bring my boy back in one piece.* And then she would break it to him that the play had already been made, and he would smile at her as he had last night, and ask her...

But equally likely he would have his arm around a Nordic blonde and it would be all, *Rose who?*

The last thought put a little firmness in her resolve and a twitch in her walk. Not that she cared what he did in his private life. It had nothing to do with her. One fake date and his seeing her in her sweet nothings did *not* give her any say or interest in what he should choose to do with other women.

Just as she was also free to play the field. And look at that field—or rink—jammed with big, husky hockey players. She recognised the Wolves by their red jerseys. Not that she would ever date a professional athlete. That was asking for trouble. But Plato Kuragin didn't have to know that.

She spotted Sasha. He wasn't hard to miss. When she'd asked him how she'd recognise him on the ice tonight he'd said, 'I carry the biggest stick.'

From here they all seemed to be carrying big sticks, but he appeared to be using his. On another player.

Great—she'd scored the player most likely to be benched.

The siren went and the action on the rink dissipated. There was some sporadic cheering and the players seemed to be leaving. Now she only had to get Sasha's attention.

'Rose!'

Clearly not hard to get his attention. He was gliding over. He reminded her of her brother Jackson at that age: full of energy and optimism, but toting an ego too big for his boots.

She took a deep breath and continued down to the rink as if she hadn't a care in the world. There was a scattering of spectators, mostly die-hard Canadian fans, and Rose was aware she had become a person of interest as she approached the Wolves' goalie. She leaned against the stanchion at the end of the penalty bench. Sasha opened the gate and approached her, tugging off his helmet.

'I will get into trouble for this,' he said, not looking too worried.

He sat down to remove his skates, his angelic face puffy with heat and sweat. Rose propped herself opposite him against the boards and asked a few non-essential questions about the game, then leaned in and told him he'd saved her bacon.

'The Wolves don't own me,' he said—with more bravado than reality, Rose suspected. 'I do it for *you*, Rose.'

Looking around to avoid having to answer such an obvious line, Rose realised a few of the other players were gliding over and wondered if the ban was off.

'I need to talk to your management,' she explained quickly to Sasha. 'They need to countersign a piece of paper that gives me rights to your face for the five minutes it'll be flashed around the greater Toronto area.'

He shrugged. 'Coach is coming over. If he yells too hard at you, Rose, I make with the protection.'

Her face softened. He really was a sweetie. The coach, however, looked mean. Okay, that meant the ban *wasn't* off. Rose straightened up and plastered on her best 'I'm Just a Little Southern Woman on a Mission' smile.

The other players were coming up against the sideline, grinning at her, talking amongst themselves in Russian. Rose watched Sasha's face and she could guess what they were saying. Hey-ho—as long as they weren't saying it in English.

Then a stream of Russian came her way that sent Sasha pale and the other players scattering, and she guessed the coach *wasn't* commenting on the shape of her ass. She was glad of the extra height, courtesy of her high-heeled boots, as she faced down a short, angry man who was definitely yelling too hard. He had a whistle dangling from around his neck. She wondered if he'd use it on her.

'It's no use,' she interrupted crisply. 'I can't understand a word you're saying.'

'You're *out*!'

Rose blinked. 'I'm not on the team, Coach, you can't bench me.'

Maybe making with the funny wasn't the right strategy. The coach went slightly red. No, definitely not the strategy.

'Listen, there's no need for all this.' She stepped closer, extending her hand. 'I'm Rose Harkness. We haven't been introduced.'

Coach stared at her hand. Then he said something about her breasts that a lady really shouldn't have to hear. In any language.

Rose stepped back, wedging her hands on her hips. 'Now, Mr Medvedev, I've read the coach's code of ethics—'

'You get out of my stadium. You get out of my team. You are interfering with play—with the bosoms and the writing on the hand and the hanky-panky.'

For crying out loud… Fair enough, she *had* inked her number on the boys' hands, and she was willing to let the crack about her girls slide, but what was it with these Russian men insinuating that she was running some sort of sexual service for lonely foreign athletes?

'I most certainly am not!' she defended herself, hands now soldered to her hips. 'Your blasted game is over, the other team are probably in the showers, and you, Mr Medvedev, are holding *me* up! I want to talk to someone who can sign off on Sasha Rykov doing a sweet little favour for me. There's no hanky-panky involved, I'm not going to besmirch the Wolves' wholesome image, and quite frankly you ought to thank me. Tomorrow, when half the population of this fair city turns on their favourite breakfast programme, there will be Sasha Rykov—and there will be thousands of women trying to get into tomorrow night's game. In fact, you really ought to print more tickets.'

'*Nyet,*' drawled a familiar voice, 'that would be the equivalent of printing money, *detka,* and the Canadian government have some laws against that.'

CHAPTER SEVEN

ROSE turned and looked up—and up. For a moment she felt as she had last night, when he'd swung her off her feet and taken her breath away.

Shoot! His arms were folded, and his whole body language screamed, *I own the world and you're trespassing.* He was wearing some sort of sheepskin-lined coat that just made him seem huge. Not that she didn't enjoy that about him; being rendered tiny and tender and feminine by your date wasn't a bad thing. Being rendered all those things by a big bull you were trying to keep roped and tied at least until you had two signatures on a slip of paper was a problem.

She also registered there were no Nordic blondes in sight, which she told herself didn't concern her.

'Oh, good,' she said brightly, 'it's the big bad wolf himself.'

The coach looked at her in something akin to shock. Sasha stopped leaning on the boards and Rose noticed the other players moving off. She'd seen this type of behaviour before; it usually happened just before a herd of cattle ran a stampede.

In that case it was probably best to get out of the way. But when had she ever done that?

'I'm trying to explain to your coach here that I'm not a danger to his precious team. I'm just trying to get a little business done.'

'Your business you take somewhere else!' shouted coach.

Rose glanced up at Plato. How much skin would it be off his

nose to come and put in a good word for her? That was if he *had* a good word. Last night she'd let her temper get the better of her, and instead of persuading him to help her all she'd done was ruin dinner and put a kybosh on anything else.

Still, she looked up at him hopefully, keeping that temper firmly reined and wishing she'd eschewed her warm pink parka for a slinky top that showed off her assets—because, really, if he wanted female skills maybe it wouldn't hurt to give him a little of what worked.

Blast. She was losing the moral high ground fast.

Belatedly she remembered the business and why she was here. All the trouble she'd taken, all the hopes she'd pinned on it. But then there was this man and the way he made her stomach flip-flop...

She gave it a last go. 'Think of me as free publicity, Mr Medvedev. It doesn't cost you anything, and I promise not to compromise Mr Rykov's virtue.'

Plato unfolded his arms and extended his hand.

'Give me your bit of paper, Rose. And I won't hold you to the thousands of women.'

For a moment Rose was rolled by the thought that she might be at fault here. She might have misjudged him. If she thought about it, he was doing what he imagined was in the best interests of his players. Until last night he had known nothing about her, and casting her mind back she realised she hadn't given him a chance to reconsider the blanket ban on his players contacting her.

All she had heard was the word *no*.

When she probably hadn't been very far away from hearing yes.

Fumbling with her bag, Rose settled herself on the players' bench. 'It's just in here. I won't be a moment. It's very simple. I don't think you'll need to have anyone legal run their expertise over it—'

She looked up, official vellum sheets in her hand. Plato took them, his eyes warm with amusement but also something else—an intensity that shortened her breath. Rose could feel a flush starting to move up her chest, but she couldn't forestall it and nor could she drag her eyes away. Pesky sexual attraction, she thought, her mouth running dry.

He gave his attention to the document. 'Pen?' he said crisply.

Rose thought he was speaking to her, but the coach handed over his clipboard. Both the coach and Sasha were observing the rink, the seats, one another—everything but her—and there was a strange atmosphere, as if everyone except Plato was embarrassed. Right now Rose was feeling a little pressure. 'I think I should tell you Sasha has already shot the commercial. We did it this afternoon.'

Plato said, '*Da?* What happened to Denisov?'

'Cold feet,' said Sasha casually.

Rose stared. 'You *knew*?'

Plato shrugged. 'If you'd hung around over dinner last night, *detka*, we could have cleared it up.'

Rose felt herself blushing a little. Did he just have to announce to the world they'd had dinner? Even if she was just a little bit pleased he wasn't hiding it.

'I should thank you, then,' she said coolly.

There was a pause. 'You haven't thanked me, Rose?'

'No.'

Plato handed the clipboard over to the younger man. 'You still want to do this, *bratan*?'

Sasha shrugged. 'Why not?'

Plato's dark eyes took up with hers again, and his mouth tilted in a half smile. 'I've been saying the same thing,' he said, and Rose got the impression he wasn't talking about Date with Destiny.

If one of her clients had reported a man's approach as being 'Why not?' she would have thrown up her hands and immediately lined up new prospects. Which made the thrill that raced up and down her spine completely and utterly wrong.

Repressing a smile, Rose retrieved her contract and replaced it in her handbag. She smoothed her hair and cleared her throat.

'Thank you very much, gentlemen. It's been a pleasure doing business with you.'

Plato gestured to the bench. 'Take a seat, Rose. Rykov, hit the showers.'

Medvedev muttered something in Russian, and Plato grinned and replied in the same language. Rose watched cautiously as something passed between the two men and the coach actually smiled.

'What did you just say about me?' she demanded as the older man ambled away, refusing to sit down and let the king of the world dominate her.

Plato gazed down at her, all thick lashes and firm mouth and broody testosterone.

Rose tried not to lose ground just thinking about how that mouth would feel pressed to any pulse-point on her body.

'I don't appreciate being discussed in another language in my presence when we both know you said something sexual about me!'

She rushed all her words out whilst keeping her eyes hovering somewhere around shoulder level. She was feeling a little embarrassed but she didn't want to admit it. If he was *saying* sexual things, she was certainly thinking them—and up until this point in her life she hadn't been that sort of girl at all.

Not that she didn't think sexual thoughts—of course she did. They were just never this graphic and not about one man in particular. The man who happened to be standing in front of her.

'I did not say anything sexual about you,' he said tautly.

He actually sounded offended.

'Sure you did. Your coach is obsessed with my bosoms, and he thinks I'm running some sort of sexual service for athletes. As for you...'

'*Da*, Rose, what *about* me?' He sounded interested.

Why didn't you call me? She cringed inwardly at the teenage girl she had once been choosing this moment to come out. Honestly, this man was in Toronto for a few days and she was supposed to be rebuilding a life for herself. This wasn't part of that picture—or was it? Funny ol' matchmaker *she* was—single and alone. But all of a sudden none of that seemed to matter all that much.

'You wouldn't let me get dressed last night,' she said uncomfortably.

There was a brief silence. 'Rose.' He was suddenly very close, and his hand curled under her chin, nudging it up so that she was forced to look at him. 'I thought we'd had our little discussion about your underwear.'

'I don't remember,' she lied, moistening her lips.

'Just now I told Coach you were a force to be reckoned with, and that you could teach the Canadian officials a thing or two about getting the best deal out of us.'

Rose rolled her eyes. 'You think my daddy raised a numbskull? Yes, right. And I'm sure you mentioned my female assets.'

'Not a word.' He pressed his thumb briefly to her lips and then dropped his hand away.

Their eyes met and a smile bracketed his mouth appealingly. She dropped her chin and laughed.

Suddenly everything felt a little too intimate. A little too much like the beginning of something...

Plato's head shifted. He lifted the tiny headset he had connected to his shirt collar and listened. Rose made out a blur of sounds. His eyes never left hers but his expression grew tense.

He pulled out his cell. '*Izvenitye*, Rose, I have to make a call. I'll make it brief.'

He walked away from her, big shoulders shifting as he moved, those long powerful legs taut beneath the cling of faithful dark denim. He took care of himself, that was for sure. *He could take care of you too,* a little inner voice murmured, and Rose cursed her suddenly very active libido.

He was walking back towards her, closing up the phone. His expression was shuttered.

'I apologise, Rose, there's something I have to take care of.'

His eyes didn't leave hers as he retrieved a card from his

inside pocket and slid it between her index and middle fingers. She noticed he didn't release her hand.

'This is my personal contact number. At eight o'clock tonight a car will pick you up and bring you to me. I've leased a house on the lake. We can resume the dinner that was so unfortunately rent asunder last night.'

He exerted the softest pressure on her hand, lifted it to his mouth and brushed his lips over her fingers folded around his card.

'Which was, of course, entirely my fault.'

He released her and gave her one of those killer smiles, and it took Rose a few moments to realise he was waiting for her response. She had one. She just wasn't sure it was anything he would understand. She didn't quite understand herself. She had never been in receipt of quite this much controlled male intent, and it rendered what should be insulting incredibly enticing. She struggled to hold her defences in place. The only thing keeping her from melting in a puddle at his feet was his assurance that she was his for the night.

'Can I walk you to your car?'

He sounded so formal her defences did a little slip-slide, because he was being such a gentleman…even as he insulted her intelligence.

'No, you go,' she said slowly. 'You do what you need to do.'

He hesitated infinitesimally but Rose made herself smile nonchalantly, put a hand on her hip, playing up to the expectations he seemed to have of her for all she was worth because she had her pride. But deep inside her something she didn't know had been unfurling curled itself up again.

She turned away and looked down at the card in her hand. How many contact numbers did a man like this have? she wondered.

Apparently only one.

She swallowed hard, wondering if this was the number he gave all the women he lined up for a little light entertainment on a tour. She knew what sending a car meant, and he hadn't even been subtle about it. She might not have had much romance in her life, but that didn't mean she'd given up on it completely—nor was she going to drop her standards.

Her hands dropped away from her hips. All of a sudden acting on her passionate nature with this man seemed a little too like getting in way over her head.

Rose came home to twenty-four yellow roses.

Rita Padalecki had brought them in when the delivery had arrived.

'You weren't home, Rose,' said the little note, 'so I used my key. Twenty-four roses, dear. He's thinking of you.'

Rose sat at her kitchen bench with a coffee and stared at Plato's card. Just his name. In Cyrillic. She traced the ink with her index finger, wondering if he had written it. Possibly... probably. She doubted the local florists were literate in Russian.

He was thinking of her. Without Mrs Padalecki's note and understanding of the language of flowers she would never have known that. She would have thought he was greasing that slippery pole he expected her to go sliding down.

A house on the lake and dinner. Bed.

He wasn't even picking her up. He was sending a car.

She scowled, and then her face crumpled because for a moment there with him this afternoon it had felt close to something...

But she couldn't go on that date. Even if he *was* thinking of her. This was clearly his *modus operandi*. She knew his reputation. She was just a face in a crowd to him, and she knew what kind of girls he dated. The non-permanent, non-stick variety.

She picked up the vase of roses and transferred it to her study, where she wouldn't have to face temptation. Then she thumbed in his number. He picked up almost immediately.

'*Da*, Rose.'

The sound of his growly Russian voice threatened to buckle her knees. She leaned against the door frame between study and hallway.

'I don't think dinner is a good idea, Plato. It's not something I'm interested in. Please don't send a car for me.' She took a deep breath. This sounded awful. 'You've been so kind helping me out, and I really do appreciate it, but I'm not really your kind of gal.'

She had expected him to interrupt her, but there was silence on the other end.

'I hope the Wolves win tomorrow night,' she said inadequately, and then pressed 'end' and flattened the cell phone against her lips.

If she stood very still and kept her mind blank this awful feeling of having thrown something important away would subside.

Rose jumped when her cell buzzed almost immediately. She closed her eyes, tried to bring down her anxiety levels before she answered. But when she looked at the screen she realised it wasn't Plato.

'Phoebe.'

Several of her girlfriends, two of whom also happened to be working part-time at Date with Destiny, were going out for drinks tonight at a new bar downtown to celebrate the future success of the business.

'Okay—yes. Sure.' She heard herself agreeing to it even as a tiny voice whispered that he might come round, might just turn up...

Oh, honestly, Rose. He hasn't called back. He's not going to come. It's over before it began.

No, much better to go out and just get on with things. Except...

When she was eleven her brother Cal had put her on her first bull calf. She'd been scared half to death but she'd known better than to show it. The little brown beast had thrown her first buck. She'd barely stayed on more than a few seconds. The longest three seconds of her whole life. Dusty and battered, she'd been scooped up from the dirt and made to promise not to tell Dad. She'd nodded, dirt on her face, a graze on her cheek, through tears she refused to shed. Her other brother Brick had told her she was pretty brave for a girl. She'd felt ten feet tall.

Right now she felt about an inch high. *Rose Harkness*, she thought with an odd little pang, *when did you become this scaredy-cat?*

The bar was noisy and full of executive types. It really wasn't Rose's sort of thing at all, but her girlfriends seemed to enjoy it. Her deep, dark little secret was that she liked honky-tonks and places where they knew your name and your daddy, and if a guy hit on you he kept it polite because he knew there'd be consequences.

Maybe this was why she was still single almost two years after she'd arrived in Toronto. She dated, but nothing with a view to the future. Not that she was in any hurry. Getting yourself disastrously engaged to a man twelve years your senior barely a year into college, having your life taken over by his ambitious family and your sexual self-confidence rubbed into the ground under his fake cowboy boot heel could leave a girl gun-shy.

But it did have a certain irony, given she had spent her whole life matchmaking. An accident on the ranch had left her motherless at six years old, and she had spent her eighth summer plotting to bring her father and her new teacher together. Through fate, her brother Cal falling off the roof and an overnight stay at her teacher Melody's house, all of Rose's work had come to fruition. Dad had been married in the fall and from that moment on Rose had been hooked.

Tomorrow morning Date with Destiny would be flashed around Toronto in a high-profile way. Her website would have more hits. Phoebe and Caroline, her girlfriends who worked on the site, would be hooking up new clients, she would continue to consult in private practice and life would go on.

And suddenly it all seemed rather…empty. Because she would still be alone.

She knew she had to take her own advice to others: be brave, take chances, allow her heart freedom. But it was hard. Bill Hilliger had taught her to doubt herself. Whilst her brothers had been overbearing at times, they had never made her feel inferior or unable to make her own decisions.

Looking back, she could see how very young she'd been— a girl with no experience of the world, of men and relationships. She had been not much more than a child with a head full of romantic notions. She gave herself credit that her belief in love and the importance of romance hadn't died with those lessons Bill had taught her. She knew better. She knew she was worth more than that.

A man across the bar was trying to get her attention and Rose swivelled on her seat, smiling blankly at whatever Caroline was saying.

'Another mocktail, Rose?' Phoebe yelled in her ear.

Rose flinched and nodded, although she hadn't finished the one she had.

Why had she come tonight? She could be with Plato. And if he wasn't big on romance he still had a lot to offer a girl… She was a red-blooded woman after all. Why shouldn't she acknowledge that and act on it?

If only he had taken the trouble to come and get her himself.

And there was the rub. She might be responding to him on a physical level, but she had deeply ingrained notions about romance and being wooed.

Even so, last night Plato had ticked some pretty significant boxes in that department, and it had made her think… Well, she knew it was old-fashioned, but she was an old-fashioned girl—she wanted to feel as if she were special to him in some way, not just a face in his crowd. For a couple of minutes there he'd made her feel pretty special…

Right now she felt as if she had her nose pressed up against the glass. Was she always going to be on the outside, looking in on love and passion? Always the fairy godmother to other people's love stories? She'd been telling herself for a little too long now that she wasn't in any shape or condition to risk herself to a serious relationship... When, really, had she *ever*? It had never been serious with Bill. She'd chosen him because he'd been exactly the sort of person she was never going to lose her head over.

Shoot! Rose's tummy bottomed out. Was that what she wanted? For Plato Kuragin to get serious about her? He was rich and high-flying and everything a Texan girl like her with down-home values should be running from. From what she could discover he dated very beautiful, flashy girls. Yet despite all their beauty and worldliness it seemed he hadn't been serious about one of them. Which raised the question: why the heck should he get serious about *her*?

Rose bit her lip. It shouldn't encourage her but it did. The story of her parents' courtship was famous in their parts. Joe Harkness had parked his boots under the bed of just about every available woman in three counties before he'd walked into the Fidelity Falls diner, sat down and ordered from a new waitress by the name of Elizabeth Rose Abbott and his life had changed. It had been love at first sight. Sometimes it could happen like that.

Rose slammed her drink down on the table.

She'd quit without staying around for the fight!

Before anything had even started she'd given up!

Her brothers would be disgusted with her. Even if you *knew* you were going to end up tail-first in the dirt, covered in dust, you had to mount up.

She'd just taken a look at the size of that bull and turned tail like a little girl in pigtails.

She jumped to her feet.

'Where are you going, Rose?'

'What's going on with Rose?'

'Hey, Rose, what about your drink?'

She pushed her way through the 10:00-p.m. crowd. She knew where she was going.

On the pavement outside she hailed a cab, and in the backseat she called Plato's cell. It went to messages.

'Plato,' she whispered, 'call me.'

Was he busy? Had he left his phone? Was he screening?

There was a huge percentage chance she was never going to hear from him again.

But as Rose slid her cell back into her glittery little bag she felt exactly as she had the first moment she'd laid eyes on him.

Like a rookie bull-rider taking hold of that long, braided rope for the first time, just waiting for the chute to open.

CHAPTER EIGHT

PLATO tugged on his cuffs and pushed open Rose's little gate.

The elderly lady he recognised from his last visit looked up from snipping her camellias.

'Hello, there,' said Rita Padalecki. 'You're back, then.'

'Good morning, Mrs Padalecki.' Plato stopped and nodded formally.

'She's been busy this morning. Lots of banging.'

Plato's mouth twitched. 'I'll have to see if I can be of any assistance.'

'You're a big, strong lad. I'm sure you can.'

The door was open. He walked on in. 'Rose?'

He could hear a vacuum cleaner upstairs. He took the stairs by threes, followed the cord into a bedroom where Rose was busily thrusting the head of a vacuum under furniture. She was barefoot and wearing the softest long-sleeved grandfather top, its tails flirting with her wide, round bottom so lovingly cupped by the same tight jeans he'd seen her in yesterday. Her hair was pulled back with a spotted red kerchief.

The last time Plato had seen a woman cleaning a house it had been a good fifteen years ago, and that woman had been his grandmother. Not the woman he had been fantasising about for the past forty-eight hours. Usually those women were wearing a great deal less than Rose. But not one of them had the effect Rose had on him dressed from neck to knee.

Why the sight of that round bottom shifting with the thrust

of her body backwards and forwards struck him as sexually provocative he couldn't have said, but it told him this was only going to end one way. He had tried to ignore it, because this girl was so far from his usual playing field it would have been the right thing to do to walk away before he started anything he couldn't finish. Even driving over this morning he had told himself to keep en route for the airport. Protect her from himself. As she had tried to protect herself in that odd little message she'd given him last night over the phone.

But he was here, and the line he'd fed himself as he pulled up opposite her house—that he had just come to say goodbye, maybe they could hook up next time he was in town—as he'd climbed the stairs, knowing she was only a few steps away, had broken down.

One look at this warm, curvy woman and she'd shoved all his excuses sideways. Even separated from her by several feet he could feel the vibrancy that was alive inside her. He hadn't imagined it. It was all there, burning hotter than ever. He told himself he was just going to warm himself against the fire that was in Rose before he went out into the more prosaic world of deals and cold-blooded decisions. Just a little taste and he would go…it would be unfair to her to ask for anything more…

He leaned down and yanked the cord.

The vacuum died and Rose straightened up. *'Shoot!'*

'Rose.'

She literally leapt, dropped the vacuum nozzle, and clapped a hand over the vicinity of her heart.

'Lordy, Plato, give a girl a fright, why don't you?'

Her eyes were huge and her mouth was trembling, although he couldn't tell whether she was trying not to laugh or cry.

Her face was scrubbed clean of make-up but her cheeks were red from exertion. Rosy, he thought, and something squeezed tight across his chest. She looked rosy.

Then his gaze dipped. The grandfather shirt was unbuttoned, so that he had a shadowy glimpse of a whole lot of cleavage, and as she stepped towards him her breasts sort of swayed ever so slightly under the soft, clinging cotton jersey. Her large, soft, amazingly rounded breasts…

How old are you, man? Thirteen?

'Well, cowboy, does a girl have to ask twice?' she asked a little breathlessly, all eyes.

She looked so wary and hopeful and knocked off-balance he just couldn't help himself.

He knew he should say something. You just didn't walk in and grab a woman. You were supposed to have a modicum of sophistication in these situations…

He stepped over the vacuum—if he'd been thinking straight he would have noted the novelty factor in *that* act—put his hands around her soft little waist and hauled her in.

Two days of anticipation hadn't prepared him for the full impact of Rose's made-for-sin body. He hadn't known what breasts and round thighs and a whole lot of woman was going to do to his self-control. Now he knew, everything went a little blurry with lust.

But first he needed to do the gentlemanly thing. He dragged his hands off her body to frame her face—her lovely, big-eyed, pert-nosed, lush-lipped face—and lowered his head.

She came up on her toes to make it easier for him.

Her kiss was soft and questioning. He couldn't blame her. She hadn't had the last couple of frustrating nights he'd endured, or the rousing sight of her vacuuming under her bed.

But he had.

As their mouths touched, slid, fused, he opened her up and delved inside, exploring the sweet taste of her, the softness of those ruby lips, hearing the little sounds of approval she made deep in the back of her throat that vibrated against his mouth.

Perfect. Goddamn perfect.

She tasted like sunshine.

And sweet, dark liquor.

He deepened the kiss.

Rose reached up and wound her arms around his broad neck. In a minute she'd stop kissing and demand to know what he thought he was doing, just walking into her house unannounced when she'd spent a sleepless night wondering if he was ever going to call. But that was in a minute. When they stopped.

The kissing...

Lordy, the kissing.

She rubbed herself up against that big hard chest, hooked her arms over his shoulders and virtually climbed him, so he was forced to splay his hands under her bottom and she had nowhere to put her legs but to wrap them around his lean hips.

'*Chert*, Rose.'

She'd surprised him—but not for long. Within seconds she was flat on her back on her newly made bed with two hundred pounds of lean, muscle-packed male bearing down on her. This was new...

He probably really could take his hands off her bottom now, but he didn't seem inclined to do so and Rose wasn't complaining. She wasn't sure if she was rubbing her pelvis against him or he was doing it himself with those big hands, but... Oh, my Lord, he really was happy to see her—and now she knew he was built to scale.

Feeling a little heady with it all, female power surging along with happy chemicals, she reached down and explored him through expensive denim—big and hard, like the rest of him.

Plato went still as a rattler just before it struck.

'Holy Hell, Rose,' he breathed, and grasped her hand and eased her off, returned her hand palm-down to his taut belly. 'You need to slow down, *dushka*, or I'm not going to last.'

He was breathing hard, and Rose took it as a compliment. She grinned at him and Plato looked a little thrown, as if something about all this was not what he'd expected. Maybe in his world girls didn't take the initiative? Which didn't make a lick of sense. For a moment her confidence gave a little under the weight of her past. Clear as crystal she could hear her ex-fiancé Bill giving her fledgling sexuality a beating. 'There's something wild in you, Rose. No man wants a wife who can't control herself.'

She darn well *could* control herself. She could control herself around Bill and every other good ol' boy who thought the woman he'd married would settle in like a mare at stud whilst he got on with his career and his carousing. Not that Bill had ever caroused. He was too uptight for that.

She just couldn't control herself around *this* particular man.

Wasn't that supposed to be a good thing?

She let go of him and lay back against the pillow, feeling all sorts of confused. Maybe she'd read the messages wrong? It wasn't as if she was in this situation every day of the week. Or the month. Or actually even the year. And really she wasn't just the sum of her erogenous zones, and she'd only just met him, and wasn't he only passing through…?

'Don't stop, Rose,' he told her, capturing her chin in his hand, forcing her to look into his eyes as if he knew her thoughts had gone galloping off in the wrong direction.

She blinked.

'Just slow down a little, *malenki*,' he assured her, his voice an octave deeper than she had ever heard it.

The sound thrummed through her senses as if he were plucking every pleasure string in her body.

'Okay,' she replied breathlessly, not sure what she was agreeing to. 'Slow…'

A rueful smile softened his eyes, and he was looking at her as if he'd never seen her properly before. She realised she hadn't thrown him at all. He looked intrigued.

'It's all about the journey, Rose,' he told her in that deep, dark voice of his. 'I want to make this good for you. There's no rush to our destination.'

What that journey would involve and where it would end wasn't clear to her, and Rose wanted to tell him that if he touched her she didn't think she could slow down. All the pleasure points in her body were so sensitised she was beginning to ache. But he was softly fingering the ebony curls lying in the curve of her throat, and it was crazy but she could almost sense him thinking.

'You are so incredibly beautiful. I want to appreciate every inch of you, *malenki*,' he said, almost to himself, in an accent that had thickened progressively since they'd hit this mattress.

And Rose believed him. She not only believed him, she wanted to go on this journey with him...

'Cowboy, you say the sweetest things.'

He was so big and strong, yet that only made his hands in her hair seem incredibly gentle, pulling her kerchief loose, running his fingers through the silky curls, making her scalp tingle. She reached up and spread her own fingers through his sun-streaked brown hair. It was so thick, and surprisingly soft. It made her feel she'd discovered something about him no one else knew.

Her eyelashes fluttered closed as his mouth dipped over hers again. Maybe this slowing down was a good thing. Yes, definitely good...

Rose got a little lost in the kissing, the nipping, the grazing, the tasting. She could feel his hands under her shirt, rucking it up, and she smoothed her hands over his back, feeling the shift of muscle, the heat of his big body.

All the while she was subtly moving against him, her jeaned thighs wrapped around one of his. This was like the making out you were supposed to do as a teenager, but she'd missed out on it.

One-handed, he pulled her loose and stretchy top down to expose a pale shoulder and a portion of her practical beige re-inforced bra that in all the sexy goings-on she'd forgotten all about.

Darn!

Plato made no comment. His thumb was pushing under the thick workaday strap, working it down her arm until he'd exposed the fulsome curve of flesh pushing up above the top of her bra.

'Your skin, Rose,' he groaned, his breath hot against her flesh as he laid open-mouthed kisses over the plumped-up upper slope of her breast. 'It's like fresh milk.' He seemed to be describing her to himself as he dragged the ugly nylon a little lower. 'And you taste so good.' Another hot kiss. 'And you're so soft...so incredibly soft.'

Was she? Rose thought she'd die if he didn't reach her nipples soon. She began to make little breathy noises she didn't recognise as her own. He was nuzzling the deep valley between her breasts, growling her name. A moan escaped her and she decided sexy lingerie was overrated anyway.

Vaguely Rose became aware of another voice calling her name. Not one of those pesky ones from her past, telling her she was behaving like a wanton, rolling around on her bed in broad daylight with a man she'd only known forty-eight hours, giving him access all areas to her girls. No, this one was a little more immediate, and it seemed to be coming from her downstairs hallway. In fact it sounded as if it was coming up the stairs...

'Oh, my Lord!' She lifted her head like a Setter sensing a change in the wind.

She fought to sit up on her elbows, still half wedged under Plato's big, pulsing body. She was breathing hard, and she was aware that her hair was all over the place and she probably had stubble rash all over her cheeks and chin and chest.

'It's Rob,' she blurted out. 'One of my clients.'

Plato said something not very nice in Russian and rolled off her.

Rose propelled herself out of bed. Or she would have if her legs hadn't felt like jelly.

'You stay here,' she ordered, patting down her hair, pulling her top back into some sort of order.

Rob was in the stairwell, his eyes lighting up as he saw her.

'Sorry, Rose. The door was wide open so I came on in.'

'Um...did we have an appointment?'

'Not exactly, but it was a nice day and I was passing.' He climbed another two stairs. 'Were you taking a nap?'

In any other circumstances Rose would have paid attention to this being a weird conversation and her barriers would have all been in place. At his last appointment Rose had picked up on inappropriate boundary issues with this man, and clearly she hadn't been wrong. Except right now she didn't much care about his problems. She needed him out of her house.

'I think you need to go, Rob,' she said a little airlessly, walking towards him with her arms held out to shoo him down her stairs. He was a tall man, or Rose had thought so. But after a couple of days' exposure to Plato he seemed almost slightly built. She didn't feel threatened by him.

She knew the moment Plato appeared because Rob lost a lot of colour.

Blast, she should have locked him in the bedroom. Telling Plato to stay put was kind of like issuing orders to a killer shark. It was best just to stay out of the water altogether.

'Who are you?'

Plato's tone of voice was one he had never used in her hearing, and Rose lost a little ground herself as she looked from Plato to Rob and then back again.

It wasn't just a question. It was a threat and a statement of ownership. His shirt was open, his hair was rumpled, and those Slavic eyes of his were narrowed, his mouth a firm, drawn line of aggression. He looked mean.

Rob retreated a step, then another. 'I'll return when it's more convenient, Rose.'

Plato just kept coming, brushing past her without a word and literally driving Rob down the stairs.

Rose knew it was cowardly to just stay where she was. She could hear Plato speaking in that low, menacing way, but not a squeak from Rob. It was out of bounds for a client to just waltz in like that uninvited, without even an appointment, but Plato was being more than slightly territorial—which the woman in her was enjoying immensely even as the professional in her head told her she needed to intervene.

Following him downstairs, she found him standing on the doorstep.

His expression was grim. 'Get your passport.'

'Wh-what? Where's my client?'

'Likely Alaska,' Plato responded coolly. 'Do all your clients just walk in off the street and go on up to your private quarters?'

'No—only the big, bossy Russian ones.' She settled her hands on her hips. 'Now, before you go any further, cowboy, you and I need to have a little talk.'

'*Da*, we talk. In the car. Get your passport, *detka*. I'm taking you with me.'

'Hold on. Taking me where?'

'*Moskva,*' he said shortly, as if it were obvious.

'Moscow? Are you out of your cotton-pickin'...?'

'You will spend a few days with me. It will be nice for us.' He slid his hand around her waist, casual as you like, and she had to tip back her head to look him in the eye. That pesky woman inside her was doing a major melt.

'What about the match tonight?'

'I must return home. I was on my way to the airport when I detoured here.'

Rose blinked in receipt of that little bit of news. 'Detoured?' she repeated slowly, the melt temporarily on hold.

'*Da*. I couldn't resist.'

He smiled at her, his eyes reflecting everything they had been doing upstairs in her bedroom. Everything she had been happy to do until she'd realised she was only a *detour*.

'How incredibly fortunate for me,' she said, her voice at chiller level. 'That explains why you didn't bother to call me first.'

Plato shrugged. 'If I'd called you we would have had one of those boring conversations about why you felt compromised by having dinner with me. I would have driven around. We would have ended up in bed.' He brushed a lock of hair from her face. 'I like you, Rose. I want to be fair to you. You have your life here. I live—there. But I find I'm liking you a little too much to resist. So we fly to *Moskva* and see what happens, yes?'

Rose sifted through all those extremely male assumptions and decided that one, Plato Kuragin had an amazingly strong sense of entitlement, but being gorgeous, rich and sought-after he probably had a lot of stuff to back that up with, and two, he was far too arrogant for his own good.

A little *Thanks, but no thanks* would help him look at those issues.

"You're so bossy," she said instead.

"*Da*, and you love it, *detka*."

She did. She was enjoying it far too much. Plato was being utterly outrageous, expecting her just to up and follow him across the world, and she really shouldn't be so compliant. She'd fled Houston vowing she would never let other people make her decisions for her ever again. It made no sense to let Plato Kuragin call the shots now…except for the thrill it gave her. She liked it. She liked the way he knew what he wanted and went after it, and how he seemed to know what *she* wanted too.

It was as if all those longings to let loose and behave wildly, repressed during her college years with a passive Bill, were rising to the surface, stirred up by proximity to this big, dominant man.

Sure, her life was here, and his was there—as he'd put it so succinctly—but how often did a guy like this appear on your doorstep? And, goodness, she liked him an awful lot. It was just that she got the impression Plato also *liked* a whole lot of other things. Namely, his comfort, getting his own way, and clearly—from the tabloid reports—Nordic blondes and Scandinavian skyscrapers. She really needed to ask him about that orgy on the yacht…

Then it struck her. For all his rather liberal sex life had been so colourfully reported over the last few weeks in the tabloids, he had been the one to slow things down upstairs. He had also been amazingly tender with her, and incredibly hot.

If she gave way to his wishes—and something told her she would—what would happen then? It was the not knowing, she suspected, that gave her such a charge. It had been so long since she'd felt comfortable enough to let a man take the reins.

It's not just him, she thought, startled, *it's me. I'm chang-*

ing. I feel confident enough to know I can snatch back those reins any time I see fit.

This was her chance to let go of being the fairy godmother and step into Cinderella's glass slippers.

Rose moistened her lips. 'I think my passport is in my desk drawer, but it's a mess. It might take some time to find it.'

Plato's big hand slid down her hip, over her bottom. 'I will help you look.'

'Somehow I don't think that's going to speed up the process. You go and explain to Mrs Padalecki that I'm going away for the weekend. She'll be concerned if she doesn't see me coming in and out.'

'I think I am already having far too much to do with Mrs Padalecki,' commented Plato, but his hand moved away and Rose found she could concentrate a little better.

'What time is the flight?' she asked a tad breathlessly over her shoulder as she padded barefoot down the hall. She couldn't quite believe she was doing this.

Plato frowned. 'Rose, we won't be flying on a commercial plane. *Malenki*, I have a jet.'

'Oh, yes. Of course you do,' Rose said, rolling her eyes. 'What was I thinking?'

CHAPTER NINE

PLATO glanced at the delicate profile of the woman sitting beside him, his hand tightening around the wheel of the Ferrari. She had such a soft look about her, and it was playing havoc with his more cynical side. Did she know what she was getting into? For that matter, did he?

The intensity of whatever this was between them made what should be a straightforward weekend in Moscow feel more like a leap into the unknown. He'd been telling himself since he issued the invitation that this didn't need to be anything other than about right now. He'd give her a taste of Moscow... him...and send her home happy. *Da*, she was a traditional sort of girl—but not so traditional she hadn't leapt into this car with him.

A more knowing hardness entered his eyes. He could put his conscience on ice. Rose was a smart girl. She'd proved at every turn she knew what she was doing.

She had her laptop open on her knee and was intent on the screen. He would have preferred her attention on *him*. She was saying something about Sasha's ad being up on YouTube. He smiled to himself. She really was proud of this little internet business of hers. Another reason she wouldn't want to be away too long...

'Clever. It won't do Rykov any harm.' He paused, then decided it couldn't hurt to tell her. 'He'll be signing with an NHL team tomorrow.'

'You're kidding?' A big smile broke across Rose's face as she turned to him. 'That's fantastic—or is it? It means he won't be playing for the Wolves.'

'No, it's great news,' he responded, trying not to get too distracted by that smile. 'He deserves it.'

'Doesn't it ever bother you? Training up these great players and then losing them to Canadian and American teams?'

'No, that's the point, *malenki*, that's why I do it. Take Rykov. He comes from a town without much to offer a kid. He's not academically minded. He probably would have ended up in the mines with his father. But he's got this skill. He can play hockey.'

'It's a way out and up,' said Rose. 'I get it.'

He glanced at her again. She was a smart girl. He liked that about her. Beautiful and smart and…funny. He really liked the funny. He wondered idly what her reaction would be if he told her what *he'd* come from, how he'd made his own way up and out. Would she judge, or would she respect the outcome? He caught the drift of his thoughts. Why in the hell did he care? He wouldn't be seeing her again after this weekend.

'Wait a minute.' She turned those big blue eyes on him. 'Did you factor all this in when you let Sasha loose on me?'

Da, smart. 'I would have given you a couple of players regardless, but I have to say when it came to making the choice of who to send your way Rykov's future was at the forefront of my mind.'

'I wish you'd told me that at dinner,' she said a little awkwardly, surprising him. 'I wouldn't have lost my temper. I'm sorry for calling you names and making threats and…other things.'

Was she apologising to him?

Plato shrugged. 'And missed the fireworks? I enjoyed it, *malenki*.'

Rose beamed. 'Sasha was my first choice anyway. I forgive you.'

Yes, she was every inch a woman. Making absolutely no sense whatsoever. And now it was his fault again.

'Excellent news,' he said.

'So is that your story? Was sport *your* way out?'

'No. I played, but it was never in my future.'

A poor boy from a mining town, destined to a life of crime to survive. How did you explain that to a girl like Rose? You didn't. That was the short answer. As far as most women were concerned he was the sum of his parts, able to give them what they wanted in the short term. It was all about *now*.

In the process of reinstalling her laptop in its case at her feet, Rose looked up at him, a smile spreading across her face, deepening her dimples.

Plato jerked his attention back on the road as the car drifted slightly. Did she have the slightest idea what she did to him? Probably, his cynicism intervened. For all that down-home charm Rose laid out, it was clearly a distraction designed to smooth over what lay beneath her surface: a fiery, passionate young woman clearly prepared to take what she wanted. He'd seen her in action at the press conference, and she hadn't been shy to make her own sexual demands this morning. He could still feel the confident glide of her hand taking his measure.

Da, she wasn't a shrinking violet, and he liked that. It was a big part of why she was with him now.

'How about you, Rose? What's in your life?'

'What would you like to know?'

Star sign? Favourite colour? How long until she dropped this country girl act and allowed the real Rose out to play...?

'I guess workwise I finished my supervised internship in Houston two years ago,' she said brightly.

Work—*da*, she liked to talk about that. 'What is this internship?' he asked patiently.

'It's part of the degree course you do to qualify as a psychologist—kind of like a medical resident. You have to earn your dues. Long hours and not much pay.'

'You are a psychologist?'

'Why, yes.' Rose looked at him curiously. 'Should I be amused or offended by how surprised you sound?'

Plato grinned. 'I was distracted by the fact you were writing your cell number on my hand, Rose.'

She looked a little uncomfortable. 'You needn't make it sound indecent.'

Indecent? His English was excellent but every now and then Rose's idioms had him paging through the Oxford English Dictionary he'd drilled himself in during his teens, when he'd come to realise language was one of the keys to a better future.

She had a way of choosing an old-fashioned word and it was a distraction. It sent his thoughts down a different, softer path. He almost believed she hadn't meant it to be a provocative act, rounding up twelve elite athletes and pressing her pen to their palms.

'I wasn't the one wielding the pen, *detka*,' he observed dryly.

She lifted that round little chin of hers as if determined to brazen it out. 'Not very professional, I know, but it got the job done.'

There it was again. The sweetness.

Da, it had got the job done. She'd taken him by surprise on that rickety old bed, and he wondered if that was part of the job too. Had she targeted him from the first? He didn't mind a bit of feminine manipulation, and Rose had already proved herself perfectly capable of it. It didn't fit, though. The whole walking into her house, throwing her onto that bed and making out with her like an eager adolescent this morning had been driven by him. Even if she hadn't left that message on his phone last night he would have stopped by. Nothing bar a natural disaster would have stopped him pulling up outside her house this morning.

Which troubled him—because he couldn't remember the last time he'd been this susceptible to a woman. She wasn't his usual type. Not that he really knew what that was. Maybe it was the little roadblocks she'd thrown up. Women usually made it pretty easy for him, and nothing about his pursuit of Rose had been easy thus far.

Rose's enthusiasm once he'd had his hands on her this morning had been a nice surprise. *Da*, very nice. And he was hard again now, just thinking about it. Where the hell he'd got the idea to slow things down he wasn't sure…although deep down he suspected it had something to do with Mrs Padalecki and the open door, and the damn vacuum cleaner and the essential sweetness he had sensed in Rose from the start. Yeah, he really liked the sweetness. Except it troubled him. What if the country girl was the real Rose after all?

'I don't mind not very professional,' he said, his voice a little husky. *Chert*, he didn't want professional at all. He wanted her mind off that business of hers and focussed on the good time he was going to show her. Instead he found himself saying, 'How did you get into the matchmaking business?'

'All I wanted to do since I was a little girl was get married.'

Plato wondered if he'd groaned aloud. How in the hell had he got himself into this? If he had a working brain cell left he'd turn this car around…

'I'm kinda famous at home as a matchmaker,' Rose continued cheerfully. 'I mean, I was doing it there before I made it my profession. I matched up my daddy with my favourite schoolteacher when I was eight years old.'

She glanced at him and began to laugh, the sound so sweet and infectious he couldn't not look at her. She bit her lip. 'Your face. It's okay, cowboy. I'm certainly not looking for a husband, and even if I was you wouldn't be it.'

'Excellent news, *detka*.'

She gave his shoulder a little shove. 'You don't have to sound so pleased about it.'

'I'm devastated. Is that better?'

She gave him a wise look and opened her handbag, retrieved her lipstick and began to apply it using a little compact, chatting as she did so. Telling him about her practice, her private clients, her hopes to open an office in the city for Date with Destiny once it took off.

Everything she said spelt out her intention of building a life in Toronto, hammering down his certainty that this was just a weekend out of her busy schedule. Plato began to relax, to allow himself to enjoy her again.

There was a lot to enjoy. Somehow Rose had turned the simple application of lipstick into an erotic act with a few slow strokes, a little rub of those lips and the barest hint of her pink tongue over the gleam of her teeth. Plato felt his body respond with predictable speed.

'How did you end up in Toronto?' he asked, his thoughts pleasantly engaged by those ruby lips.

'I stuck a pin in a map.' She grinned at him, as if knowing how unexpected that sounded. 'I hit a riverbed, but Toronto was the closest major city, so here I am. There's a young population, the dating scene is surprisingly diverse, and I saw an opening for a marriage brokering business.'

The dating scene? Plato's imagined use of those sweet lips came to a screeching halt as he had an unwelcome flashback to Rose sashaying around that reception room with her little bag and curving ruby mouth, moving from athlete to athlete until she turned those big blue eyes on him.

'You date a lot, Rose?' His virtual growl brought her head around in surprise.

'I do my share,' she said with a little shrug.

What in the hell did *that* mean? He caught the dawning look of uncertainty in her eyes and tamped down his unwarranted surge of jealousy. What on earth was wrong with him? She was a beautiful single woman in a populous city. It would be impossible for her to step outside that front door of hers and not trip over a line of eager guys all ready to do whatever it took to take her to dinner…to bed.

Just like him.

'How in the hell are you still single?'

'I don't know how to answer that,' she said, looking a bit taken aback.

He couldn't blame her; he had no idea why he was making a big deal out of this. *His* reputation was hardly spotless.

Rose tried to think of something to say, because she *did* know how to answer him—it was just he would never believe her.

She thought of her teenage years when she should have been dating, the victim of four well-meaning, overprotective big brothers. Years she'd spent matchmaking for other people instead. Then had come her college years, when her social life had consisted of dinner parties, fundraisers and functions on the arm of the wrong man—a man she'd chosen specifically to avoid her brothers' interference. A man who along with his family had bullied her and chipped away at her self-esteem until her confidence in herself as a woman had been at an all-time low. Her gradual climb back to normality over the last couple of years had been hard, until now she could date and socialise like any other girl. Yet somehow she was still single.

She wasn't about to tell Mr Bored, Built and Between Blondes any of that. Except she wasn't really thinking of him that way any more. He was Plato to her now. Plato with the gentle hands and deep voice and protective instincts.

'I'm very busy with work,' she prevaricated, which made a mockery of how easily she'd dropped everything to leap into this car with him. Nor did he look convinced.

'*Da*, the destiny date,' he said slowly, as if considering it. 'And you make a comfortable living from this?'

It was a sore point. 'Not really. I have a small client list I brought from the practice I worked in when I first came to Toronto and I see them on a private basis. It pays the bills.'

'You prefer this matchmaking?'

'It's an honourable profession.' She hated the defensiveness she could hear trickling into her tone.

'You like happy endings?'

'I like to give people the tools to make smarter decisions

about who they love,' she corrected, telling herself he wasn't being patronising. Telling herself not to lose her temper. She'd already done too much of that around this man.

'*Da*, you believe in fairy tales.'

'That goes to show you know nothing about me,' she retorted hotly, losing her temper anyway. 'I can assure you, Plato, I know personally how ugly the relations between men and women can be. I choose to educate, not to feed people fairy tales.'

'What is this ugly?'

Rose folded her arms. 'I don't want to talk about this. You clearly don't take my work seriously.'

'Who has mistreated you?' he demanded abruptly.

'I was speaking generally, not specifically,' she prevaricated, looking away.

'You said personally.' He spoke over her. 'What is this personal?'

'None of your business.' The speed she had begun to take for granted had dropped away, and Rose realised in horror he was pulling over onto the shoulder of the road.

'For land sakes, Plato,' she squeaked, 'what are you doing?'

He cut the engine and angled his body to face her. 'Who has mistreated you?'

It must be a cultural difference, thought Rose, backing up fast. This macho, looking-after-my-woman thing. Except they did it in Texas too, and her romantic disasters could all be traced back to it.

'Plato, I really don't appreciate being strong-armed like this…'

In the silence, the stillness, Plato was suddenly right there, examining her as if looking for signs of domestic violence. This was silly. Except he looked so fierce…and concerned.

Well, heck…

'I was engaged to a man for four years. We had our problems.' She moistened her bottom lip. 'I guess you could figure that, seeing as I'm not with him any more.'

'What did he do to you?' His voice was low, tough.

'Do to me? Kind of what you're doing now,' she muttered.

'Sto?' Fine lines bracketed his eyes, and his slanting Slavic cheekbones lifted as his face drew taut.

'Putting on the pressure.' She fidgeted, opening and closing the clasp on her handbag. 'Look, this is my personal business. I hardly know you well enough to—'

'You said ugly,' he cut in. 'Naturally I am concerned.'

Was he? She looked into his eyes and her heartbeat stumbled.

Rose Harkness, don't you go falling down a mountain over this man. He's big and overbearing and you may as well never have left Texas if you do!

'It's as boring as watching paint dry,' she grumbled, opening up her bag. 'But here we are, if you're so darn curious. This is as ugly as it got.'

She thrust the folded segment of newspaper at him. Never taking his eyes off her, Plato unfolded the paper. He flicked his gaze over it. Rose knew the headline by heart: 'Fidelity Falls Beauty Queen Throws Over Hilliger Heir.'

The text was brief and to the point.

William Randolph Hilliger III, son of Senator William Randolph Hilliger II, loses pre-selection and fiancée overnight. Miss Harkness was unavailable for comment.

'I've read about *your* past in the tabloids this week,' she said, endeavouring to inject some normality into her voice. 'Well, here's mine. All five minutes of my fame.'

'Tabloids? You researched me, *detka*?' She was about to deny it when he said, 'This is you?' The hint of a smile softened the line of his firm mouth. 'Miss Dairy Queen? How old were you in this picture?'

'Eighteen.' She'd been plumper then, and the long dress had been too tight, but the sash hid the worst of it. Her hair had been styled into a sixties beehive. She was posed on the back of a hay truck.

'Cute,' he said, handing the cutting back. 'So who is this Third?'

'Bill,' she said firmly, 'was a guy I met in my first year at college in Houston. I hadn't dated much before then...actually I hadn't dated at all.' She saw the look on his face and hurried on. 'I come from a small town—Fidelity Falls, like it says in the article—and I've got four big brothers. It kinda made things...tricky.'

Understatement, Rose.

'All I wanted to do since I was a little girl was get married,' she told him again, and then broke off, looking a little flustered. 'I'm not doing this right. I'm explaining it wrong.'

'Keep going,' said Plato.

The smile she kept glimpsing was starting to bother her. She knew how it must seem to him—the small town, the pageant picture, the early engagement. Country bumpkin. But she wasn't going to hide where she came from. Not any more.

'Even in college my brothers interfered in my romantic life. They chased away any boys my own age who showed an interest. So when Bill came on the scene nobody suspected a thing, because he was so much older, came from an established Houston family. Who'd think he would be dating a college student? Worse, a girl from Fidelity Falls?'

She risked a glance at Plato. He wasn't smiling any more. He looked stone-cold serious.

'I was able to sort of sneak around with him, and I guess it made it exciting. I hadn't had much excitement in my life of the romantic kind.' She sighed. 'He wooed me.'

'What is this *woo*?'

'Courtship. You know—he sent me flowers and took me to dinner and on picnics, wrote me poems.'

'Poems?'

'Later I found out he'd had a staff member of his father's write them, but at the time it seemed...romantic.' Rose shook her head. 'I was very young, I thought that was how it worked. Men and women. But now I know different. He took my romantic notions and he trashed them.'

Rose risked a look at him. Plato's smile was long gone.

'Bill's daddy was a senator, and all the Hilligers go into politics. Bill had a whole big career lined up—except he didn't really have the heart for it. I think he would have been happier lecturing in politics for the rest of his life, but his parents insisted he was bound for big things. He wasn't very confident with people…with women. I guess he chose me because I was so young and naive. He proposed a month into dating me, and I said no, but he kept asking, and by that time his mother had taken me under her wing and my whole social life seemed to be caught up with the Hilligers. Everyone around me seemed to expect it.'

She closed her little bag with a snap.

'It wouldn't have been so bad except he tried to make me ashamed of where I came from, of my family, and for a time I was. He tried to change me.' She gave Plato a big false smile. 'So you see—blinkers off. I'm a tough cookie these days.'

'Da,' he said slowly, 'you're a tough little biscuit. This guy—why did you stay with him so long?'

'One minute I was living in a dorm with other girls. The next I'd moved into his house, was going with him to dinner parties and functions, living a life beyond my years. I guess I didn't know how to step off the train.' She broke off, realising she was almost wrenching the strap off her bag. 'The idea was we would get married when I finished my degree and had a bit more social polish, and Bill would put his name forward for pre-selection. I started volunteering at a women's shelter as part of my degree. The Hilligers weren't happy about it, and that was when I first said no to them. Then I just kept on saying no—until one day I told Bill it was over. I was twenty-four and I'd grown up. In the end I worked out that he just wanted a woman on his arm who wouldn't embarrass him in public. Which is ironic, because that's exactly what I ended up doing.'

Plato nodded at her handbag. 'You dumped him. Why was it newsworthy?'

'Only in Houston. The Hilligers are big news there, and I used to get dragged along to all the functions with Bill. I made the mistake of agreeing to go to a political dinner after we'd broken up, and he used it as the venue to announce our wedding plans. I guess he thought he could strongarm me that way into doing what he wanted. I caused a little…scene. The press were there and it was all over the next day's papers. It was a Sunday. Slow day.' She patted her bag. 'I carry it around with me so that it doesn't become some sort of deep dark secret. It's yellowing now. I imagine in a few years the print will be so blurry I'll have to throw it out. Which is how it should be.'

'Take what you need and move on,' he said quietly. 'Smart. This small town you come from—you didn't go back?'

'I became the girl who threw over the Hilligers instead of the Dairy Queen. I couldn't go back and face that.' She made sure her tone was light, almost flippant, keeping a tight hold on the emotions memories of that awful time always evoked. 'I had my degree by then, so I packed up my suitcase, stuck a pin in a map and came to Toronto to start my own life.'

She gave him a wry smile. 'I guess you want to turn the car around and take me home now,' she said with a nervous little laugh. 'Talking about old boyfriends isn't very sexy.'

'*Detka*, everything about you is sexy,' he assured her, but there was something behind the easy smile he gave her that made Rose wonder if she'd said too much, made herself seem foolish to him.

CHAPTER TEN

So ROSE had had a little unhappiness in her life? She'd clearly bounced back. She was a smart, capable woman. She didn't need him riding in like some sort of Prince Charming, slaying her dragons.

Yet as he pulled out onto the highway Plato glanced at her serious, downcast profile and something hot and tight moved through his chest.

'Where in the hell was your father or those brothers of yours when all this was going on?' he demanded roughly.

Rose looked up, blinking with surprise. 'I protected Bill from them, of course,' she said simply.

Plato swore under his breath.

Rose sighed. 'I don't want to talk about this any more, but Bill wasn't like...well, you. He hadn't had all that much experience with women. I guess I liked that about him. He didn't overwhelm me. In fact if anyone was the aggressor it was probably me.'

He glanced at her again, and to his surprise Rose cut her eyes away. She looked a little embarrassed.

'You went after him?' He could hear the scepticism in his own voice.

'No, I mean—' She broke off. 'Never mind.'

But he did mind. He was feeling angry and protective and he wanted to kick this guy who had taken advantage of a young Rose to the kerb.

It was completely unreasonable, but Plato found himself wondering where he'd been all those years ago. In the Caucasus mountains shooting insurgents, trading illegal car parts on the black market. Not fronting up and sorting out Rose's life for her. *Chert.*

Rose, a Texan beauty queen who didn't date and had hooked up with an older guy because she wanted to get married. *Da,* she was a traditional girl all right.

Realising his knuckles had whitened over the steering wheel, he purposely began to dial it back. Rose could have been a cliché, but she'd managed to break free of all that and forge something for herself. She'd turned her own longings into a paying business and she deserved respect for that, not his misplaced desire to fix things for her.

She wasn't that eighteen-year-old Dairy Queen any more, for all that she carried a little bit of newsprint around attesting to it. She was a grown woman and she knew the score.

His role in this little scenario was to take her to Moscow, show her a good time and make sure—for her comfort and his—she didn't get under his skin. She didn't need a guy like him messing around in her life; from the sounds of her story what she needed was a little fun.

This is about sex, man, and it's time to get this show on the road.

After her confession Rose was trembling like a leaf. Being so honest with another person had left her feeling exposed and vulnerable, raw. Plato was quiet. He drove and she stared uncomfortably out of the window and tried to fathom why in the heck she'd turned a simple get-to-know-you into a blood-and-guts confession. Talk about killing the mood.

To Rose's surprise her big Russian didn't drive into the airport terminal car park. He kept going, hung a right, and drove to some fenced gates. He lowered the window, handed his pass to a guard and they drove on through. Rose realised they were driving towards the tarmac.

Holy cow.

She stared up in sheer amazement.

A whole lot of shiny white, black-detailed jet, with a red and black wolf's head design on the cockpit. It was the equivalent of this car. Except so much more.

'It looks—fast,' she said inadequately.

'You like speed, *malenki*?'

Rose shook her head, trying not to let her nerves show. 'Not me. I'm strictly third gear.'

'Slow it is, then,' he assured her, bringing the car to a stop.

Plato flipped the ignition, removed his belt, reached over and unfastened hers. Before she could move he slid a hand around her shoulders, drawing her towards him. She had a moment to register he was going to kiss her and then his mouth was on hers, hard and fast, his tongue rough and ready and rhythmic, taking what he could get. His other hand tangled in her hair as he cradled her head, angled her for a better penetration.

This wasn't slow…

Rose heard herself moan, felt her hands going helplessly up to his shirtfront in an effort to touch him, find a little skin, bond herself to him. Vaguely she intuited that he was giving her some kind of message with this kiss—a kind of *This is what we're about, baby, and don't you mistake it for anything else.* After her little tell-all soap opera confession she was lucky he hadn't dumped her by the side of the road.

Then just as suddenly his hands eased their hold, and he was smoothing the hair away from her face as his mouth turned softer, sweeter. She clung and looked at him dreamily as he drew back, his eyes very dark on hers. For a moment he looked a little thrown.

'We need to move, *detka*,' he said roughly, releasing her.

Plato was out of the car and had her door open. Rose climbed out on wobbly legs and turned around to face the jet in the near distance. Her stomach dropped. Out of the car it seemed to loom even larger.

Worse, whilst they'd been kissing another car had rolled up. A couple of guys were getting out and were openly watching her with Plato.

The cold wind snatched at her long A-line skirt. Rose was wearing a high-necked wool sweater and a jacket but the wind knifed through it. Wrapping her arms around herself, she turned towards Plato and said helplessly, 'You could have given me fair warning.'

'I was occupied,' he imparted with a flashing smile. 'It's just Security, *detka*. I apologise. I forget you are shy.'

Was she? Rose didn't think she was particularly shy. Just private about…private things.

He shrugged off his coat and wrapped it around her. She was instantly enclosed in the lovely musky male scent of him, faintly tinted with an expensive aftershave. He slung an arm around her and, casually as you like, steered her across the tarmac.

It was like something out of a movie. Rose kept expecting a director to yell *Cut!* or *Print!* and her big, gorgeous-as-all-get-out Russian to transform into a sexy stranger and lope away. Because she hardly knew him, did she? All she knew was that the backs of her knees gave a little every time he smiled at her, and right now she was enjoying being the centre of his attention so much it was seriously going to hurt when he took it away. Because people always did, and with a guy like Plato that moment was probably coming sooner rather than later.

If she truly was the modern girl she liked to pretend to be she'd just enjoy it for what it was: a good time, not destined to last. But she wasn't a modern girl, was she? She was from a little town in Texas where you married your high school sweetheart and went to church and had babies.

Except she wasn't doing any of those things. She'd failed spectacularly at the lot, and so she had decided two years ago to make a life out of getting those things for other people.

It was such a depressing thought that for a moment she had to fight the urge to pull herself free of his arms and hightail it back to the airport, jump in a taxi and speed home to the safety of her own four walls, where she had built a life to replace the one she'd fled from in Houston. And it was a good life. It just wasn't particularly exciting.

The last thought brought her back to her senses. Ahead of them the jet loomed, larger than life—kind of like the guy who had his arm around her. This was real, and if it was different that was a good thing. Except she needed to settle this on her terms. She'd learned her lesson with Bill Hilliger. She might be taking a long-needed risk with this man but she wasn't his plaything.

Her eyes narrowed on that jet. Here was a good place to start. This was exactly like last night. The only difference was this time he was using a bigger toy to bring her to him.

Time to rope this bull down, Rosy.

At the foot of the mobile stairs she ground to a halt.

'I can't get on this plane with you if this is just some sex thing.'

Plato was suddenly standing right up in front of her, blocking out the wind, his face close to her own. 'Sex thing?'

He was giving her that *you're-speaking-in-a-foreign-language* reaction but she wasn't buying it.

Rose put her hands on her hips.

'You know what I mean, cowboy.'

Yes, he knew. She could see the speculation in the look he gave her, as if summing her up, reaching for the words that would seal the deal. 'I will treat you like a queen, my Rose,' he said, in that deep, sexy voice. 'You have my word.'

'A queen, huh? Just see that you do.'

A genuine smile creased his face, drawing fine lines at the corners of those Slavic eyes of his, and Rose had a glimpse of the boy he must once have been. Her heart gave an unexpected lurch.

Oh, my, that wasn't good. That wasn't good at all. She wasn't to go all soft about this guy. He was definitely not the man to let her guard down around so soon.

'All right then,' she said a little breathlessly, the wind taken out of her sails. 'Just as long as we're clear.'

Plato couldn't credit the satisfaction that streaked through him. He had her. The street-smart boy from Udilsk had scored himself a real live princess.

Da, with a fake line he'd delivered before to women who couldn't care less as long as he showed them a good time. He hadn't missed the vulnerable light in her eyes. The odd little speech she'd made when she'd called to refuse his dinner date last night flashed through his mind. *Not his kind of girl.* He wondered how much she knew about his reputation from the tabloids. She must know something. Was that the root of this *sex thing*?

He wanted to tell her he wasn't that man. He wasn't the guy who'd wanted to send the limo to pick her up when he'd known the first night they were together, when he'd barely scratched her surface, that she was the kind of girl you drove home.

Da, and what would you know about that, Kuragin? Peasant boy from a hick town. You'll amount to nothing. Everything good you touch turns black, cheap...

'Rose,' he said in a rough voice.

Her expression was pure caution, and it flashed through his mind what she'd said about how her romantic notions had been trashed.

'I will look after you, *malenki*,' he promised.

He had no idea where the words came from, but he sure as hell didn't expect what happened next. She moved so quickly he didn't have time to do much more than stand there. Rose wrapped her arms around his middle and held him tightly, communicating a whole lot of the feeling he'd been sensing all along was just below her surface.

She barely gave him time to react, even if he had known how to, because now she was letting go and scooting up those steps.

The gesture left him stranded. He couldn't remember anyone ever touching him in that way—or was it that he had never allowed it? For a moment the repercussions of what it meant silenced the usual cynical voice in his head that didn't allow those thoughts in. He gave himself permission for just a moment to wonder what it would be like to have this in his life.

Rose in his life.

Then the familiar intervened.

What is wrong with you?

She was from a completely different world. She would never understand what he had come from. If she had the faintest idea she wouldn't be here with him now.

He needed to get a hold of this.

"Coming, cowboy?" she called over her shoulder, her look pert, confident.

Da, she wanted this as much as he did. He wouldn't think about why. He'd just take what she was willing to give.

They touched down in snow. It was falling lightly but steadily. The bright lights of the building were harsh as they walked the concourse, flanked by security men.

Plato retrieved his cell, took a call.

'Rose, we are in for a bit of press attention outside. I'll get you into the car as quickly as possible, but I advise keeping your head down and using your bag to obscure your face.'

Rose frowned. 'What do you mean, press attention?'

Plato shook his head at the ludicrousness of the situation. It would be impossible to explain to this girl what a Russian businessman's life meant—especially one who had risen from the streets. She would not understand the dangers or the insatiable interest of the press. The world loved wealth and everyone wanted their piece of him.

'Cover your face,' was all he said, and Rose obediently lifted her handbag, holding it up and let him guide her steps as they emerged from Moscow's Domodedovo Airport into sub-zero temperatures and were showered in a flare of clicking cameras.

People were shouting out questions in Russian, French and English at Plato, who had his hand firmly anchored to her waist as he urged her onwards. Rose scrambled gratefully forward and was plunged into the privacy of the smokescreened limo. Plato was sliding in beside her. A minder was slamming the door.

'Are you all right?'

Plato's expression was taut as he ran concerned eyes over her. As he spoke he leaned forward. His coat was open, the broad expanse of his chest exposed in a faithfully cut olive shirt. Rose couldn't help getting a little lost in looking at him. He must work out an awful lot...

She nodded vigorously, but that nod immediately turned into an even more vigorous shake. She hadn't expected this. Cameras, attention...

She had seen the media interest in Plato back in Toronto at that press conference, but until this moment she hadn't really known. Until this moment she'd had no idea.

And right now it was all feeling a bit too much.

'Why does this happen to you?'

'Good question.' He glanced away out the window into the darkness. 'Just here, Rose, in Moscow.'

He'd been this way, a little distant, throughout the long flight. Rose knew it was to do with her hugging him. She got the impression it wasn't something he'd enjoyed, and she felt as if she'd revealed her hand too soon. If she were a long-legged, worldly-wise Scandinavian model she would probably have taken his words as her due—chivalrous, but meaningless in the larger scheme of things. But she was a plump-calved, down-home Texan girl and he had said something that in her book was romantic. Her instinct had been to hug him. She hadn't been able to help it. Probably no more than he'd been able to help looking as if someone had thrown him out of a plane without a parachute afterwards.

But he had put her first, ahead of his own comfort, and she hadn't expected that.

His gaze returned to her, moving over her with unabashed sexual speculation. Yes, he seemed a lot more comfortable with this kind of attention, and if this was where it started, so be it.

She could work with this. But at her pace. She was in charge. She wasn't that girl striving to please a man who wasn't interested. Bill had been her first lover. She knew now her libido had definitely out-powered his, but when they'd been together he'd always made her feel somehow *too* sexual—as if her wants and needs were unfeminine. Intellectually she'd known it was nonsense, but deep down in her psyche she had absorbed his distaste for her sexuality and her womanly body.

Plato didn't seem to have any problem with her body; in fact the fuller than average curve of her *derrière*, the roundness of her hips and thighs, had him all sorts of intent and interested. He made her feel sexy and kind of powerful, and it put ideas in her head. Bold ideas. She was going to be Plato Kuragin's Waterloo whether he liked it or not! He was going to fall so hard for her his knees would be ringing with the impact for years. She'd be the girl he'd never forget. The one who changed his wicked ways…

'I've got a series of meetings in the centre of town,' he was saying almost abstractedly as his eyes zeroed in on her mouth.

No more skinny blondes without bottoms…

'I'll have Ivan drop me at the Kharkov Building and take you on to the apartment.' His deep voice strummed her senses. 'I'll join you around midday.'

No more orgies on yachts… Well, she'd like to *see* his yacht… She pulled up short. 'I don't understand. It's the middle of the night.'

'You might want to alter your watch, Rose. It's just after 7:00 a.m.' He was smiling at her.

'It can't be. It's pitch-dark out there.' She forgot for a moment what they were talking about. He really did have a sensual smile. It made her think of silk on her skin and the way he'd pressed those hot kisses to the swells of her breasts. She shivered.

'It's winter, *malenki*,' he said in a deep, dark voice. 'Welcome to Russia.'

Thinking about what this welcome might actually involve, Rose asked faintly, 'When does it grow light?'

'Around nine. Don't look so worried, Rose. You can get settled in, take a nap, put on something pretty.'

This was sounding disconcertingly like instructions. On how to seduce him. Rose found she didn't mind.

'But what about you? When do you sleep?'

'I'm like New York City, *detka*, the lights never go out.'

Rose took in the male confidence, the humour, the deep sexual speculation in his rain-dark eyes and decided she was going to be the one lining *him* up. She took a breath and dived in.

'Okay, cowboy, if you're New York City that makes me upstate; we *do* sleep and we keep regular hours. I don't know if three or four is going to be enough for me.'

'I will call you.'

Rose unsnapped her bag. 'Have you got my number?'

'I will phone the apartment…' He stopped, the expression on his face worth the fool she might be about to make of herself.

Smiling to herself, Rose retrieved her little gold pen and scooted across the seat. 'Give me your hand.'

'I cannot believe you are doing this,' he said, but his voice had dropped an octave and as she inked the numerals she could feel the heat and solidity of his big, hard body close to her own. The temptation to cuddle in and hope for the best was intense, but a little wooing on his behalf wasn't going to go astray.

'There we are.' She capped her pen and bent her head to blow lightly over the wet ink.

Plato said something under his breath.

'It's just my number. I'm not promising anything.' Rose lifted her face with a half-smile. 'Call me.'

'I am thinking my meetings can be cancelled,' he growled.

Rose put her pen away and shut up her bag. 'No, I think you ought to keep your appointments. A girl needs a little upkeep after such a long flight. I want some proper food and some fresh clothes and oh, definitely a bath. A nice warm bubbly bath to soak my poor attenuated limbs and other…' she made a sweeping gesture down the centre of her body '…girly bits and bobs. And I certainly don't need you for that, do I?'

Plato looked appreciably absorbed in what she was saying. Rose had the feeling that if a stampede of cattle came through the limo he wouldn't notice anything but her. She turned up guileless blue eyes to his lambent grey.

His voice was killingly deep when he spoke. 'You play with fire, Texas.'

'Well, you think about me playing with fire and I'll think about you doing…whatever it is you do.' She let her eyes linger on his big, hard body.

It was a bold move, but being polite and waiting her turn had never got her anywhere in life. She'd done plenty of that in Houston, jamming the real Rose down where she wouldn't cause any trouble for Bill Hilliger and his family. She was long over it.

Plato silently reached across and closed the privacy screen.

Rose gave him her sweetest smile, even though her whole body had begun to tremble.

'You're not going to kiss me, are you, cowboy? Because this is neither the time nor the place.'

He looked amused and disbelieving. 'When *will* be the time and the place, Rose?'

Rose knew this was her moment to seize the reins. Be the cool, sophisticated woman who held all the cards instead of the hot, hormone-driven girl who was pushing the cards off the table and landing in his lap.

But when she met his eyes she was confronted with hooded sexual dynamite. He was looking at her all moody and brooding, as if weighing up his options with her.

Rose moistened her lips. They felt swollen and incredibly sensitive. All the dating advice she'd ever offered had been predicated on waiting, getting to know one another, shared interests… This was moving awfully fast. If he kissed her now they wouldn't be stopping, she thought faintly, heart pounding, and had she really come all this way to be tumbled in the back of a car? Then she realised the car had stopped. Had probably been stopped for a while.

'Ivan will take you to the apartment,' Plato instructed with a slight smile, as if he knew what she'd been thinking. His eyes did that lazy, satisfied thing all over her body. 'You can settle in, freshen up.' His charismatic smile flashed at her. 'Have your bath.'

Rose suddenly really wanted to drag him into that bath— waiting be damned. Except he was opening the door of the limo.

"One more thing, Rose," he said seriously. "I don't want you to answer the door to the apartment, and once you're inside don't go out."

"I don't understand."

"Just do as I ask and there won't be a problem."

Then he was gone. He didn't try to kiss her, and he didn't even say goodbye…after taking away her choices and issuing orders.

Rose pulled herself upright, her knees knocking together as the car pulled away from the kerb.

Her mind blank, her stomach stone-cold.

CHAPTER ELEVEN

ROSE gazed meditatively into her glass of tea as the savoury pastries called *piroshki* the waiter had recommended went cold on the plate. Her appetite had left her at about the time Plato had issued orders in the limo, placing her under house arrest.

Except she wasn't in his house. She'd walked into his apartment and taken one look at the stunningly designed rooms, absorbed the fact of the money it had taken to create something like that and felt like the unsophisticated farm girl from a small town the Hilligers had always painted her to be. Worse, all of a sudden all she'd been able to see were the parties the tabloids said Plato was famous for holding there, the blondes she had read about who had been in his bed. She hadn't even been able to find his bed, and once she'd found herself looking for it Rose had lost patience. She'd stamped her foot, jammed her arms into her coat and marched out of that apartment with her head held high.

Which had brought her here, to a restaurant adjoining the gallery at the end of his street. She'd spent the past hour drinking tea, calming down, and trying to figure out what to do.

This is where your hormones get you, Rose Harkness, she grumbled to herself. *Halfway across the world and at the beck and call of another big, bossy man...thinks he can tell you what to do...wants to treat you like his little sex doll...locking you up in his apartment...*

Her thoughts skidded to a halt. This wasn't about being controlled. It was about her own fears. Because Plato wasn't trying to change her. From the get-go he'd accepted her on her own terms. In fact she got the impression he enjoyed her standing up to him. *She* did. She liked bumping noses with him. She liked it a little too well.

Oh, heck, she wanted to give this a chance. Except to be with a man—this man in particular—she was going to have to open herself up to being hurt, maybe to being loved. To the whole drama. To the possibility of loss.

Three seconds on the bull, Rose? a tougher little voice intervened. *Is that going to be your lifetime record?*

But she was scared. None of this was about what had happened to her in Houston. This was all about her deepest fear— the one that had left her wide open to a guy like Bill Hilliger. The death of her mother and her father's retreat into grief. No room in his heart for anyone—even a small girl who had no one else. She had seen what happened when love was taken away. It had been taken away from her too. She was so afraid of falling in love and having love taken away she had chosen a man she would never love, and in the process she had idealised the notion of finding that one special person. She'd built a business around it! And because of her fear she needed that special man to be perfect before she took a chance.

Plato sure as heck wasn't perfect.

Mr You-Stay-Indoors-and-Stay-Put certainly wasn't perfect...

But he was just about everything she'd ever wanted. A man who swept her off her feet and looked at her as if she'd been invented just for him, who seemed to relish the fire in her. And sometimes in life you had to take a chance.

She was willing to take that chance with Plato, but right now, thinking about the apartment and the parties and the blondes, the orders and the fact she was sitting here alone, she was getting the real impression that the only risk *he* was taking was an alteration to his busy schedule.

* * *

Plato entered the down-lit environment of the private bar off
Ulitsa Svobody, scanning the tables, the look of the place,
satisfied by its lack of pretension. From outside you wouldn't
know it was here, and yet it did the best business of any of his
bars in the city—had done since its opening six months ago.
It was closed right now.

He'd spent the better part of the morning talking to his board
and fielding questions and now he was about done. He needed
to touch base with Nik Stolypin, old friend and second-in-
command, and then he was going home for some recreational
activity with his little import from Texas. So far, so normal.

*Yeah, keeping telling yourself that and maybe you'll be-
lieve it.*

Nik walked away from the employees he was talking to,
opening his arms wide as he approached.

'*Bratan*, good to have you back.'

'Good to be back.' The two men collided in a bear hug that
spoke of their long partnership.

'Coffee, yeah?' said Nik, making a gesture to the guy pol-
ishing the rails around the five-metre length of the bar. 'Saw
last night's game. The Wolves pounded them.'

'That's what we were there for.'

'I heard about the Sazanovs. Shame.'

'Rykov's gain.'

'The NHL have signed him up instead, I heard?'

Plato shrugged off his coat onto the back of a chair and
leaned up against the bar. One of the screens was broadcast-
ing a soccer game.

Plato glanced around. 'The bar is looking good.'

'Four more of them opening around the city,' said Nik with
some satisfaction.

Plato picked up one of the espressos set down on the bar,
idly gave a little attention to the game on the wall.

'I also heard our guys were tearing their hair out when you
fronted at Domededova without the team.'

'Yeah, well, it doesn't hurt to keep them on their toes.'

'What in the hell were you doing, putting them on a commercial flight instead of taking them in the jet?'

'The girl I was with wouldn't have been keen on a crowd. It was simpler.'

'Plato Kuragin disrupted business to accommodate a woman? Right. Who is she and what has she done with my best mate?'

'She would have been uncomfortable; it was the right thing to do.'

Nik rocked back on his heels. 'Who is she, man? Why are you being so cagey?'

Plato stirred on his feet. He didn't know quite why he was so reluctant to talk about her. Nik was his oldest friend. There was a lot of water under that bridge. He settled on 'Her name is Rose.'

'Rose? Pretty. Old-fashioned.'

Old-fashioned, *da*. He smiled into his drink.

'English?'

'American. From Texas.'

'Model?'

'Matchmaker.'

'Yeah, right.'

Plato shrugged, continued to watch the game above the bar—although right now it wasn't making much sense.

'You're not kidding, are you?'

'She's got this little business—' Plato broke off, found himself smiling ruefully as he rubbed the back of his neck. A picture of Rose perched on the coach's bench, rummaging in that little retro bag of hers for the contract as if it were a lipstick, sprang to mind. 'It's hard to explain.'

'Keep going. You're doing a good job. Got me riveted. Rose, a matchmaker from Texas, and it's hard to explain. You know, I'm picturing a short, fat woman in a flowery hat.'

'You keep picturing that, *bratan*.'

'You bringing Flower Girl to the party tonight?'

'Rose,' Plato growled.

Nik lifted his hands in a mock gesture of surrender. 'Rose,' he amended.

Plato didn't answer.

'Where have you got her stashed?'

A vivid image of Rose in his bath bubbled to mind, of her spreading soapy water over her... What had she called them? *Da*, her 'girly bits and bobs...'

Plato's involuntary smile made Nik give a knowing grin. 'She's in the apartment, isn't she?'

Rage blindsided him. One moment he was standing there, his mind full of naked Rose, the next she was respectably dressed and he had shirt-fronted Nik up against the wall before the other man even saw it coming. He found himself pressing the heel of his hand into his best friend's sternum before he realised what he was doing and even then he didn't let go. Not straight away.

Nik swore, shoving at him. Plato let him go, shifted restlessly backwards a few steps, shocked, still angry. What was he *doing*? A better question was what was he doing with Rose?

'I apologise,' he said roughly.

Nik was steamed. Plato didn't blame him. But he still wanted to plant his fist in his face for that suggestive crack about Rose and the apartment.

'Did you get the figures I sent through?' asked Nik, his tone devoid of emotion, all business.

Plato grunted. 'Yeah, I've been over them. Talk to Oleg. He's got the details.'

They talked about business for a few more minutes. Nik calmed down. Plato experienced an ever-growing tightening in his gut.

'This girl—Rose,' said Nik as Plato reached for his coat. 'Come tonight. I want to meet her.'

'Maybe,' he said, easing his shoulders into the wool and fur. But maybe not. Rose in his nightclub. Rose in his world. Rose finally seeing who he really was and walking away.

Women always did. A little withholding of attention, lapsed phone calls, long periods apart. *Plato, do you actually see this going anywhere?* He'd heard that line so many times he'd perfected the regretful shrug, the formal embrace, the delivery of a piece of jewellery—the pricey goodbye they all expected from him.

But his last break-up had been different, and maybe that was why she'd gone viral on the internet. He'd come back to a hotel—had it been in Berlin? He'd just had the news that his old coach Pavel Ignatieff, the closest thing he'd ever had to a father, had succumbed to cancer. All he'd wanted was a human voice, a touch—something to ease the shock and sadness. Instead he'd got what he'd paid for: a high-maintenance girl who was angry because her agent hadn't got her some photo shoot.

He hadn't been in the mood to take her out. So he'd ended it. And now he was paying the price with some notoriety he didn't want and probably didn't deserve. He wasn't promiscuous. He was twenty-eight, male, successful in an industry that attracted sexy women.

Yet it had been months since he'd been with one of them. Ignatieff's death had hit him hard, and it had thrown everything into sharp relief. The women, the lifestyle, the relentless search for something to blunt the essential truth that he didn't feel as if he deserved more.

It was lightly snowing as he emerged into the street. A car was waiting for him. Another car would follow at a short distance. Toronto had been a nice release from the sort of measures he needed to take on his home turf—especially in Moscow, where he didn't go anywhere without armed guards.

He pulled out his phone. Cold invaded every cell of his body as he read the security report in growing disbelief. Who had delayed sending this to him?

He'd put a guy on Rose to ensure her safety, and apparently he'd been right to. She had stayed approximately half an hour at the apartment before appearing in the street and taking off on foot. She'd walked a few blocks before rounding back and entering the gallery down the road, where she had been for the past few hours.

Alone.

He swore and gestured to the car.

CHAPTER TWELVE

Without her really noticing it the restaurant had gone very quiet. There was a lull in the general conversation, and even the quiet clink of cutlery, porcelain and glass had evaporated. Rose looked up.

Plato had changed clothes since she'd seen him earlier. He was wearing some kind of suit that made him look older, harder...incredibly sexy...and he was coming towards her across that restaurant as if nobody else existed.

Rose sat up a little straighter, her heart slamming against her ribs.

He didn't look very happy. Which was fine with her. She didn't feel very happy with him either.

He bore down on her. His hands hit her table and rattled the cups. He leaned in and icy grey eyes clashed with her own startled blue.

'You do *not* leave the apartment without letting me know where you are going.'

She jumped in her seat and she saw him register her reaction, because for a moment his expression softened a little as he searched her face.

'Rose, do you understand me?'

He was looming over her the same way he had the other night in her house, when he'd come storming in all suspicion and sex appeal. Except right now what she felt was a rising tide of anger—because this wasn't her problem, it was *his*.

Plato pulled out the chair opposite and dropped into it, moody and tense, framing the table with his big arms as he rested his hands on opposite ends.

She glared back at him, blocking out all the wonderful things she knew about him and making herself concentrate on the rekindled suspicion that he just wanted to control her.

'You cannot wander this city on your own.'

He was looking at her as if trying to work her out. She could have told him she was having the same problem.

Yet even as he was being completely unreasonable she was viscerally responding to the deep, masculine note in his voice, to the way he looked at her, *all* of her, as if *she* was the one being unreasonably provocative, as if she'd invented her mouth and her breasts and her hips to distract him from what was necessary right now. Pulling her into line, putting the hard word on her about who she was in his life.

Most shockingly, the woman in her was glad of it—was in her imagination unbuttoning her little jacket, one button at a time, never taking her eyes off him just so she could see him suffer a little longer, and then climbing over the table and making it all better.

Sweet bejesus, she was out of control with this man.

'It's not safe,' he said.

There's something wild in you, Rose. Bill's words came back to her. *No man wants a wife who can't control herself.*

She swallowed hard.

Damn it, I'm allowed to be passionate and sexual and happy...

'What? This restaurant?' Her voice was low and husky and...taunting. She actually saw him respond, the way his eyes went down, settled on her mouth, his features growing taut with sexual intent. Rose began to tremble inside. 'Has there been an outbreak of salmonella I don't know about?' Her joke fell flat.

Plato dragged his attention away from her to pull out his phone. He thumbed through it and laid it down in front of her on the table. Rose looked down at the screen. It was an internet image of herself and Plato at the airport. Her face wasn't completely covered by her bag and she was entirely recognisable.

Her blood ran cold.

'The company we settled on for security in the clubs announced the deal yesterday, before we gave the all-clear,' Plato said flatly. 'It's the reason the media were at the airport. I would have protected you from it had I known. But your face, Rose, is now public property.'

Every muscle in her body pulled tight. 'Will—will people see this in the States?'

How on earth did she explain Plato to her family? She couldn't even explain him to herself.

'I doubt it.' He picked up his phone, long fingers closing tensely around it.

The adrenalin surge over, she felt a little faint. A fork slipped and clattered on the plate.

'This isn't Toronto, Rose, it's Moscow, and there's a certain level of security I require—especially at the moment.'

Rose was a little thrown. Not by the security stuff—everyone knew rich Russians were super-sensitive about those things—but the fact there might be a reason why he hadn't wanted her to leave the apartment.

Relief flooded her.

'You're now included in that security until you fly out at the beginning of next week,' he continued.

He was already talking about a date for her departure.

She knew she would be going—she'd worked too long and hard building up her business to be away any longer—but right now, with everything so uncertain between them, it felt pretty lousy to be reminded of it. He'd said it himself. He was here and she was—there.

What she had been hoping up until this instant was that he would say, *Da, baby, I can do this. I've got a jet. I can fly in weekends*.

But somehow she knew that wasn't going to happen.

'I meet beautiful women all the time. Many of them give me their contact details. You just did it in an unusual way.'

'Rose, do you understand? When you're not with me you need to be where I can keep an eye on you.'

She'd only been half listening, but those familiar words, combined with the certain knowledge that this had never been anything but a hook-up on his part, brought her up short.

'An *eye* on me?'

He seemed to be grappling to express himself. 'You're from Texas, yes? The history of your country, your Wild West, this is very much the feel of my city at the moment.'

'You mean Moscow is like Dodge?' she said, a little lost. 'Except Dodge City was in Kansas?'

'Da.' He sat back, running his gaze over her as if making an inventory of her dark hair, her eyes, her mouth, the slope of her shoulders right down to her lap.

He's thinking about sex, Rose thought edgily, because she was no longer feeling particularly sexy right now. *He's weighing me up as if it's worth his while.*

'Naturally there are laws, but there are a lot of people working outside of those laws.'

'Shady types?' she said dully.

'Da, shady types.' He ran a hand over the back of his neck, drawing attention to the strain of his bulging biceps under the close-weave fabric of his jacket.

Rose wrenched her gaze away. He didn't belong to her any more. He wasn't hers to desire.

He leaned towards her, as if sensing her withdrawal, his forearms coming down on the table. He reached for her hands. 'You need to behave yourself whilst you're with me, Rose. No more of these unexpected surprises, yes?'

He had lowered his voice to an intimate level, his hands closing around hers, his thumbs rubbing her wrists. The feeling was making her breathless and sad and angry all at once.

'We don't want any more photographs of you in the papers. Can you do that for me?'

Rose dragged her hands back, her expression one of utter dismay. She felt the same way she had in that restaurant the first night, when he had revealed so casually that his players had been warned not to contact her.

As if she were Timebomb Rose, who might go off at any moment.

She'd lived that persona for four years. Having her actions monitored, having to run her decisions by another person who inevitably overruled her.

The one thing she had learned from the whole experience was that she wouldn't walk that road again, not for anybody. Not even for a gorgeous Russian who made her want things she couldn't have.

She threw down her napkin and launched to her feet.

'I'd like to go home now, please.'

And she didn't mean his apartment.

He gave her a look that was angry and frustrated.

'*Da*, we go,' he muttered, as if making up his mind about something, pushing back his chair and pulling out a billfold. He peeled off a few notes and tossed them down on the table. Five times the cost of her meal.

She wanted to yell at him and tell him she wasn't a woman he could toy with. She wasn't some game for him to play because he was bored and rich and...

She didn't really want to go home.

She wanted to give this a try...

And then it occurred to her. Plato might be a whole heap more important than Bill Hilliger and his influential family, but she hadn't really felt it until now. All the time she had spent with Bill she'd been made to feel like an unsophisticated hick, but Plato hadn't made her feel like that once.

Last time she had been in a restaurant with him she'd stormed out, she hadn't given him the benefit of the doubt, and she had been proved wrong.

Was she wrong now too?

Troubled, confused, she looked up at him, trying to sort out the old feelings left over from her years in Houston from the new ones he had stirred in her over the last few days and line them up with what was happening now. Was she ready to risk her tender heart? Would he prove worthy?

'How about we do this?' Plato said, far more calmly than he was feeling. He was used to dealing with women, their idiosyncrasies.

Rose had just shifted from her singular spot as the only girl he'd ever spent time with who hadn't bored him stupid, into the row of spoilt divas he'd handled on a regular basis for the last several years. She was just another girl who liked to get her own way and he'd mistaken that for character. He ignored the man in him who wanted to shake some sense into her and then wrap her up tight in his arms.

'I am opening a new club in Monaco mid-week. We'll fly down. I'll get you back to Toronto from there.'

He sounded bored. He *was* bored. He'd done this all before. With far too many women to number.

'Monaco?' she said a little faintly. 'That sounds—ritzy.'

All of a sudden she just wanted to cry.

She'd really hoped...what? That this would be different? With a man like this? Was he really going to put in the time to fly in and out...*date* her?

'*Da*, you can do a little shopping, we can go to the casino—you'll have fun.'

Patronising her, thought Rose, and everything she had been building up in her head about this man disintegrated into nothing. She'd been mollycoddled all her life by a father and brothers who adored her; she'd wasted four years of her life with a man who'd both controlled her and underestimated her. She wasn't wasting five more minutes on a man she had known three days who clearly had no interest in getting to know her at all!

Plato took her elbow almost impersonally, steered her across the restaurant. People were looking at them. Looking at *him*.

He was right, she thought. He wasn't an invisible man in

this city, and now he had been transformed into that silent stranger she'd imagined back on the tarmac in Toronto who would walk away.

Well, she could do it too. With a lot more class.

She wasn't going to Monaco with this man. She was going as far as his apartment and she was packing her suitcase.

Except as he helped her into her wool coat she was invaded by a sense of longing for what she had so briefly had with him, only sharpened by the knowledge that she needed to go home. He turned her in his arms, began to button her up although she could have done it herself. She let him. His expression was closed, his eyes impassive on hers.

He knew as well as she did that it was over. Before it had even started.

The physical longing for him welled up inside of her.

Wild, uncontrollable Rose.

Frustrated, and frightened by the intensity of those feelings and what they told her about herself, she suddenly needed to put some physical distance between them and she pulled away, heading straight for the doorman, who opened the plate glass doors at the entrance.

Plato swore and followed her out, his temper barely restrained. He grabbed her arm as she stepped out onto the wide snow-swept pavement, saw the cold hit her like a gravity pull. His instinct was to protect her from it. She wasn't used to it. He shoved that soft thought aside. She wasn't *going* to get used to it.

This had been a mistake—a girl like this and a man like him.

Something pulled tight and hot in his chest. He took a sharp breath past it.

She needed to go home. Whatever this was, it ended here and now.

Rose tugged her arm free. 'Let me go, Plato,' she said stonily.

He knew what she meant.

He noticed the car the moment they hit the pavement. A smokescreened Mercedes S-class idling by the roadside, its engine a low rumble. Not discreet—but these things never were.

Plato knew what he had to do, but unease shifted sinuously up and down his spine because it was going to scare the hell out of Rose. She had darted ahead, her bag shoved under her arm, and was doing her best to put some distance between them.

It all happened in a matter of seconds. The car accelerated, braked, and three men leapt out, crowding the pavement in front of Rose.

They were all in sharply tailored coats, fur *ushankas*, smiling pleasantly at her, but Rose backed up, her head whipping around, her blue eyes searching for him.

He was on her in moments, shouldering her behind him. "What is it, boys? Got lost and looking for directions?"

"You know me, Kuragin, always hunting for a new investment." Ivan Gorkov looked Rose up and down. "You need to be more careful with your property. No telling what could get damaged if we don't sort this little problem out."

"It's sorted, Gorkov. Nice and legal. So you can take your girlfriends and go and file another injunction and we'll deal with it in court."

He knew his security team was only moments away, but fronting up to a guy like Gorkov was often the simplest solution, and he didn't want this to turn into something it didn't need to be. He could feel Rose at his side, the bump of her arm as she pressed in against him. She was a tough little thing, and he didn't quite trust her not to put her own *kopek* into the mix. He knew better than to make eye contact with her. As far as these guys were concerned she was just a woman who was with him—an onlooker. He wanted it to stay that way.

Except he could hear her soft rapid breathing and it made a difficult situation fraught, because all he could think about was protecting her.

One of Gorkov's men shouldered up to him and Plato stepped forward, knowing he had to shove thoughts of Rose aside and keep pushing this. It was all about intimidation. Gorkov was a local mafia bit-player who wanted in on the club scene in Moscow. He had put in several bids to service the bars and nightclubs Plato had made his name with. This morning a legitimate security firm had announced winning the contract. Gorkov clearly had the misguided view that making his disappointment personal was going to change things.

Rose couldn't believe what she was seeing. Plato was grinning at the guy shouldering up to him, even as he kept up an almost mocking dialogue with the shorter man in the superior tailoring.

He lifted his hands in what appeared at first glance to be a placatory gesture, but his fingers curled and Rose realised in mounting horror he was beckoning the aggressive guy towards him, keeping her behind him as he moved.

No, Plato, she thought desperately.

'You cannot wander this city on your own.'

His words came back at her. This was actually happening.

'When you're not with me you need to be somewhere I can keep an eye on you.'

She had made such a terrible mistake…

There was an animalistic quality to the way the men were circling one another now, and the smiles on their faces were sending Rose's blood cold. Other people were giving them a wide berth. A couple of onlookers were pointing. Plato said something guttural in Russian and the short guy in the fur-lined coat blanched. He moved uneasily on his feet, looking left and right.

Plato kept coming, eyes narrowed, features drawn tight, and Rose realised he was fully able to deal with this. She was with a man who understood this situation in ways she couldn't begin to fathom, and whatever Plato was saying to these guys he was making his point.

They were breaking up, shifting onto the road.

Rose's stomach, tight and clenched from the moment this had started, began to cramp as she realised it might be over.

Plato beckoned to her, his eyes never leaving the men as they vanished into their car and took off. Rose didn't shift an inch. She was wobbling on her legs as it was, and frankly she wasn't sure what to do.

It was pounding in her head. *This could have been so much worse. I should have listened to him.*

Plato had whipped out his cell and was snarling into it as he crossed the few feet between them. The arm he used to drag her in against him was not gentle. Rose instinctively pressed her face into the lapel of his coat. He felt solid and hot and very male, still pumping out testosterone although they were safe now. Weren't they? With other people passing them on the street, going about their business, it all felt very normal.

'Plato—'

'Nichivo,' he said briefly, shoving his phone back into his coat.

He had put in a report to the police. He could give her his full attention. He knew what she'd seen had been seedy, dangerous, confusing to a woman like Rose. She would have questions, or maybe she wouldn't. She needed comfort and soft words and protection. He could offer her protection, but he didn't have any soft words for her. All he had was blood hammering in his head and surging into his groin. He was going to have her, and he didn't much care for her opinion on the matter.

They could go from there.

Rose bit down hard on the inside of her lip. He must think she was an idiot.

'Plato, I—'

'Rose.' He grunted her name and lowered his head and kissed her. It was a gesture designed to shut her up, and he knew his mouth wasn't reassuring.

Rose whimpered. His lips were hard, bruising. He was taking from her what he needed. His life was so much more hard-edged than anything she could imagine, and instinctively she understood he needed something softer, something only a woman could give him. Rose wasn't sure what she wanted, but she had never felt more female—because he needed her, and it was sending hot, undeniable messages to every one of the erogenous zones in her body.

She tried to kiss him back, but he dragged his mouth away and she remembered they were standing in the street, and nothing about this was private. Then she forgot that because he was trembling against her.

'Are you okay?'

Plato made a derisive sound and clamped his hands on her hips, bringing her in tight against him. Rose felt him hard and thick even through the layer of her wool coat. She knew she should have been outraged. They were in public, and she had a dozen questions, but in an instant all she was aware of was how aroused he was and what it was doing to her.

He was sending her a message. She was his to take, and this was what he wanted from her.

It was outrageous, but right now it didn't matter because it was what she wanted too.

CHAPTER THIRTEEN

ROSE thought she'd made her decision in the street, but as Plato unbuttoned her coat in the foyer of his apartment and she slid out one arm and then the other she acknowledged that that was a lie she'd been telling herself for days to hide the truth. She'd made this decision the moment she'd clapped eyes on him at the press conference in the Dorrington.

She applied her smaller hands to his coat, gazing at the broad hard chest she was undressing, and lifted her revelatory eyes to his. For a moment she faltered. His expression was so hard, and the events in the street flickered through her mind. For a second she wondered who this man was. She still had dozens of questions…

But he forestalled her questions by lowering his head even as he dragged her up into his arms, and suddenly he was completely in charge and she was…hopelessly caught up in his embrace. Rose had never felt so excruciatingly excited in her entire life.

The men she had dated in the past had always asked if they could kiss her. Sometimes she'd said yes, occasionally no. It had always been very civilized, and she'd kept the ball in her court. Like the boys who'd pursued her back in Fidelity Falls and made the mistake of going through her brothers first.

Plato's mouth took hers without a by-your-leave and he didn't hold back. It was as if, like her, he'd been fantasising about this for days. Heat exploded between them and sent a chain reaction through the rest of Rose's body. She felt the erotic intensity of the moment almost too acutely. One hand was clamped at her hip, holding her flush against him, whilst the other delved into her hair as he cradled her head and kissed her. No man had ever kissed her as Plato did, ravishing her mouth, forcing her to open to him, taking what he wanted.

Plato knew he was holding her too tightly. He had to be hurting her. He felt her wince but he couldn't *not* squeeze, couldn't *not* drag her up against him. He heard her soft, broken breaths as she struggled to kiss him back and knew he was being an unreasonable brute—but really what did anyone expect? What did *she* expect? *Chert*, she knew what to expect now. She'd had a brief blast of everything that was wrong in his life. Now she could have a taste of what it meant to mess with a guy like him.

He fumbled one-handed with the buttons on her tight little wool jacket, popping one, then another. He only stopped kissing her to appreciate the cleavage and fine black lace. Nothing beige in sight. He realised she'd put this on for him—before the argument in the restaurant, before she'd fled from him down the street, before she'd known the truth. For some reason it made him clumsy all of a sudden.

Rose pushed her hands to his chest and shimmied down to her feet, the look she gave him both inviting and wary. Her small hand did guard duty over her jacket and she backed up.

For a crazy minute he thought he'd blown it. That she'd decided it was over. The luxury of the private, privileged world he had won his place in was no longer able to screen the base realities of where he had come from. She was thinking about what she had seen and heard in the street, and like the smart girl she was she wasn't going to let some street thug from Udilsk touch her.

Rose reached up and laid her hand on his cheek, her gentle palm drawing the weight of him towards her. She was so intensely lovely, her hair falling out of its pins and framing her face in loose ebony curls. It struck him that the first time he had seen her she had reminded him of a Renaissance Madonna, but the Rose he knew now was much more earthy and real, and that fire burning inside her suffused her delicate features, making her eyes intensely blue as she gazed at him.

She came up on her toes and put her lips to his and kissed him, soft as the inside of a rose petal, her eyes wide open, never leaving his. Slowing him down.

Plato stopped moving, stopped breathing.

Rose knew now he'd only ever told her the truth, had only ever been trying to protect her, and she so desperately wanted to give him something back. From all she had seen today and what she now knew about Plato's life it seemed the thing he lacked was tenderness. She could give him this—a little softness to take the edges off his hard life.

A sensual smile curled up the corners of her mouth and she kissed him again, this time her eyes drifting closed as her tongue delved between his lips, holding his head in place with both hands. He leaned forward so Rose could reach him, and the gesture wasn't lost on her.

She could feel the lust thumping inside him. She had never been wanted like this. She opened her eyes, saw the strange wild light in his and asked, her voice pure enticement, 'Where do we go?' She wasn't entirely referring to geography.

Plato hauled her into his arms and carried her up the stairs. She put her arms around his neck and he could feel her warmth through her clothes, the female weight of her so wondrously distributed.

He lived upstairs. It was simpler, more comfortable than the vast spaces below. He saw Rose taking it all in—the pool table, the excessive entertainment consoles, the big screen on the wall, the huge sofas and walls and the ledges full of sporting memorabilia. She seemed to grow heavier in his arms, as if relaxing. He'd never brought a woman up here before. He wondered what she was thinking. Then he kicked open the door to his bedroom.

He kept expecting she would start up at him, stamp her

foot, demand to be taken to the airport… He wouldn't let her go, but he put her down and she didn't do any of those things.

Instead she began unbuttoning his shirt, her hesitant touch driving him crazy. He replaced her hands with his more competent ones, ripping, sending buttons spitting. He dealt with her little jacket until he had her soft hands on his bare chest, nothing but silk and lace and underwiring between her breasts and his skin. She reached up and tugged his head down to fuse their mouths.

He hauled her up into his arms until she was dangling. He carried her over to the bed, still kissing her, and pulled down her skirt and tights and panties in one swift movement before setting her on the bed.

Rose knelt there in her slip, eyes dazed, ruby lips parted, everything left to the imagination but the peaking of her nipples. It was a sight so incredibly erotic he almost came. Seemingly ignorant of her effect on him, she reached for the buttons on his trousers. But he replaced her hands with his own because right now the only thing that mattered was to shed his trousers and briefs, deal with the condom before he disgraced himself.

She gave a little gasp as he tumbled her backwards onto the bed, eyes wide, and for a moment he could have sworn she was a little nervous. Wordlessly he rucked up her slip, knowing he should say something, but he found the incredibly soft flesh of her inner thighs and words failed him. He tangled his fingers through the little soft dark curls at the heart of her and touched her heat. Rose moaned.

He muttered appreciatively under his breath in Russian, sliding his fingers into the hot slippery centre of her body, teasing her clitoris with his thumb, watching her eyes close, her back arch, listening to her whimper. He couldn't wait.

Rose lifted her hips instinctively and his expression grew heavier, his eyes half closing as he slid between those gorgeous milky-white thighs, nudged her heat with his erection. He sheathed himself inside her, wide and deep. He didn't pause, didn't give her any time to adjust, he just wanted to claim her.

Rose sucked in air. For a few seconds the pressure was too much. It felt almost too much to take. She moved to push at his hips, but in that instant everything changed. A streak of pleasure in the wake of the unrelenting pressure caught her off guard and her little cry of protest tapered off into a full-throated moan.

He caught her mouth with his as he began to move, slowly but mercilessly, deliciously inside her.

Oh, my Lord…

More pleasure rippled through her nerve-endings as she began to move against him, teaching him what she needed, discovering it for herself. More—definitely more was what she needed. She told him so, in desperate little gasps of instruction.

Plato thrust in answer, deep and hard, the muscles in his back rippling under her desperately clutching hands. He yanked her legs up around his hips, her ankles pressing to the hair-roughened backs of his thighs, rubbing against the muscle as he thrust into her again and again. The pressure built, and all Rose could do was sob as her body sang around his. He shifted harder and higher and sensations ripped through her—until the inevitable happened. He threw back his head, the corded muscle visible in his neck and shoulders, his biceps pumped up. These visuals swooped through Rose's mind as he grunted her name, buried his head against her neck with a harsh male groan and pulsed inside of her.

Rose wrapped him up tight in her arms as he came down on top of her, breathing hard. The weight of him…the scent of male skin and clean sweat and sex mingling with fresh linen sheets… All she could do was absorb his vulnerability in that moment and hold onto him. They were quiet together for a long time, their laboured breathing giving way to softer sounds and then a counterpoint.

'Is it always like this?' Rose murmured, shifting her head against his sweat-damp shoulder.

'Moscow?' His voice was a dark note she felt deep down in her sensitised body. 'No, that was not ordinary.'

'No, I mean this. Us.'

His fingertips played lightly over the little bumps on her spine and his eyes sought hers, that strange wild light still flickering there.

'No.' He gave a dry, involuntary laugh that sounded more like a groan. 'This was definitely not ordinary.'

No, not ordinary. Sort of magical and...

'Because I thought I'd lost you,' she admitted softly, when before she had been too afraid to form the words.

'No.' He turned to her, his expression almost fierce, his mouth hot and dry against her temple. 'No.'

'I thought you were trying to control me,' she confessed.

'*Nyet*, I want to protect you,' he said roughly.

For any other woman those would have been magic words, thought Rose.

'Like my dad and my four brothers,' she said aloud, realising as she spoke that he had been trying to protect her from outside forces as her brothers would—not to manipulate her as Bill had tried to do, trying to control her because he was weak and she was strong. Plato welcomed her strength.

'Not like them.'

He nudged her chin up so he could look into her eyes. Rose's heart gave a kick. He understood her.

'You are my woman. There is a difference.'

Well, there was that, thought Rose faintly, and found she'd run out of words.

She'd never been anyone's woman before. She was a daughter, a sister, and she had been a girlfriend, a fiancée, a friend... But never someone's woman, and there was a difference.

'I have learned today you are capable of looking after yourself.' This admission was accompanied by a smile that took her mind off their conversation and back to the warm thud of his heart against her spread hand.

'What else have you learned?'

'Not to take you out to dine. Whenever we are in a restaurant, *malenki*, it always ends in you storming out.'

'True.' Rose buried her smile in the bronze hair curling over his chest, arrowing down towards the taut musculature of his belly. Her hand followed. He was so *male*, as if every other man she'd ever met was a faint copy of this original.

Plato smoothed a hand over her rounded thigh, sliding up the silk she still wore. In a minute he'd strip it off her, learn every luscious inch of her centrefold body and anchor himself to the physical. But right now the femaleness of her body brought him back to how intimate this had been, how right it had felt.

He looked down at her face, her flushed cheeks, her closed eyes, the upward ruby curve of her lips. What was going on in that pretty head of hers? Was she judging him for the complexities of his life she couldn't possibly understand? Surely what she'd seen today in the street had shocked her, and yet... she seemed fine. She was smoothing one gentle hand over his chest as if she were offering comfort in turn, and something tightened in him.

'You will have to get used to the security,' he said, his voice a low rumble in his chest, and waited for a reaction.

Rose sighed, snuggled a little closer. After today she would be glad of ten good men and a titanium wall between her and that explosion of male aggression and intimidation.

Running her hands over her own personal titanium wall, she wondered at what that meant. *Get used to.* He had to know she wouldn't be staying here with him. It needed to be a fifty-fifty thing. She moistened her lips, knowing it was the moment to say something but unable to form the words. Did it really matter? They'd work something out. They *had* to work something out, because she wasn't giving this up.

Nothing in the world could make her give this up.

Plato eyed her carefully, trying to read her. She seemed utterly compliant, and he felt that tightening in his chest again.

'*Malenki?*' he said in that deep, dark voice, his big hand closing proprietorially around the curve of her bottom.

'Yes, cowboy?' She blinked slowly at him, feeling as if the sun had just come out blindingly after a long winter.

'Have I told you it was my lucky day when you wrote your number on my hand?'

'I think you just did.'

Yet even lying in his strong arms she could feel the wariness in him as if talking intimately with a woman like this wasn't something he had much experience of. Or maybe it was just her.

If both of them were gun-shy of taking a risk it was hard to see a future together.

She sighed as his hand began to drift again, covering her breast, thumbing her nipple through the lace. He bent his head and closed his teeth ever so gently over her now perky nipple, all rosy and pleased to see him through black lace.

He was rucking her slip up, and she lifted her arms above her head for him to ease it off. He reached under her to unfasten the tricky three hooks on her bra. She imagined he was accustomed to women who didn't need so much support. It made her feel shy and a little exposed—until he peeled the lace and satin away slowly, unbearably slowly, and his eyes told her everything she wanted to know. Because he wasn't looking at her breasts. He was looking into her eyes.

In the shower the water was warm, pulsing over her ivory skin. Her luscious, odalisque's dream of a body was climbing his. Plato's hands knew what they were doing even as his mind went to all sorts of places he didn't want to investigate, and Rose lifted herself to him, as wild for him as he was for her. For the first time since he'd arrived in this cursed city a decade ago something felt right and natural and good.

Wrapped in a towel, her hair damp and toppling over her shoulders, Rose sank onto the bed, reaching for him. But almost the minute her head touched the pillow she was out like a light.

He'd never seen anything quite like it, and he sat for a while, just watching her. Then he hooked one arm behind his head, wrapped the other around Rose, and tucked her up against him, his shoulder her pillow. She was still damp from the shower, fragrant from the shampoo and her own warm, female skin. In the shower she had tasted under his tongue like every flavour he craved. She slept in his arms as if she were a sea creature who had found her shell.

Yet he hadn't kept her safe.

No matter how many times he told himself what had happened today had been a matter of fate, they had been in the wrong restaurant in the wrong street at the wrong hour. He kept coming back to the indisputable truth that he had been hard pressed to protect her, and no matter how much security he carried there was always going to be a level of danger in this city for him. He had made enemies here; even building a legitimate business he couldn't avoid it.

She didn't belong here, and it was just a matter of time before that became clear to her too... Again he felt that odd clenching sensation in his chest.

She was safe in Toronto. He had never visited a safer city. He remembered the vital interest her neighbours took in her welfare, how she left her damned doors open in the middle of the day, how trustingly she had come with him, a virtual stranger, halfway around the world to this place.

This beautiful, historical, treacherous city, with currents that could sweep you under just like that. He knew. He knew better than most. Because he had been both under and on top, and he knew which position he liked best.

He had learned to swim with sharks to survive; he could tear apart flesh with the best of them.

Yet in his arms lay this girl who melted him.

She just did. And for the first time in his life he didn't know what to do.

CHAPTER FOURTEEN

Rose opened her eyes, pushing herself up, yawning hugely, widening her eyes as she saw Plato standing at the end of the bed in grey sweatpants that rode low on his lean hips and nothing else. Just lots of male skin and muscle, and a hazing of dark hair all over that broad chest narrowing down to his taut abdomen and lower.

Oh, my. This was the best dream ever.

She smiled, the cat that got the cream, and stretched, the sheet dropping and settling around her waist.

That ought to do the job.

'Cold chicken, salad, bread, cheese, fruit.'

He laid it out before her on the bed as if in offering to a goddess. Which was exactly how Rose was feeling right about now.

'And the *pièce de resistance*.' He grinned. 'Blueberry pie. Texas-style.'

Food winning over sex, Rose peered with interest at the pie. Gathering the sheet around her, she inched forward on her knees, inspecting her feast. She was a hungry goddess.

Plato dealt with the champagne. Rose laid out the plates and cutlery.

Plato handed her the glasses and propped himself up against the bedhead, dragging Rose onto his lap. They fed from a single plate.

'Plato?'

Her soft Texan drawl, the cadence that was hers alone, made

his name sound unfamiliar and yet absolutely right. The soft 'plah' when everyone else said 'play'. The scent of violets in her damp hair so close to his face teased his senses, and as she turned her head towards him he could see the pugnacious tilt in that dimpled chin of hers.

'What happened to you?'

He angled a look at her. 'What sort of question is that?'

'I mean how did you get from the Urals to this?'

So this was it. The inquisition that would tell her what she needed to know. He wished he could give her a story that would please her romantic heart, but all he had was the truth. He was what he was, and he had never hidden it from anyone. He wouldn't start now.

Blood, sweat and tears. He wound a long dark tress around his hand. *Luck, opportunity, making every moment count.* The usual. All of this he could have said to her—had said before in interviews.

'I won a hand in poker.'

Her expression filled with delight. 'Don't tell me—you parlayed it into a fortune?'

'No, I bought a train ticket and washed up here in Moscow. Did a load of jobs, worked security. Army service intervened. I got out, did a couple of years of economics at university, and worked nights as a bouncer.' He watched the surprise bloom on her face and the familiar coldness closed around his heart as he continued. 'I figured the guy I was working for didn't know how to turn a *kopek* into a *rouble*, and he was making a fair living from it, so I opened my own place in a neighbourhood about to turn from a slum into a growing concern and from there I expanded.'

'How did you know the neighbourhood was going to turn?'

'I was living there, *malenki*.' He watched her reaction closely, his eyes hooded.

'Oh.' She tried to picture that—Plato without the accoutrements of wealth. In her mind's eye he was still Plato. She imagined he'd been born in charge, taking names, issuing orders. She relaxed back against him. 'And now you're famous for it.'

'Free market capitalism has been very good to me.' He stroked her long hair. 'Otherwise I'd still be that tow-headed country boy playing hockey in winter and kicking a football around in summer.'

'I like to think of you as that boy. When I was a kid I wouldn't play any sport at all, on principle. My brothers always made such a song and dance about having to include me that I walked away rather than be made a fool of.'

Plato tried to imagine her as a little girl. She would have been plump, he could see that, with that cute little nose of hers unformed, and probably with her hair in pigtails and a whole heap of temperament too big for a child to handle. He wondered how her brothers had survived it.

He was more than ready to take the focus off himself. 'Tell me about these brothers.'

'Cal, Boyd, Brick and Jackson. Jackson has got three years on me, and they just go up from there.'

'I am seeing where it comes from. The attitude. You needed it.'

'Yes, well, I learned young to stand up for myself. But they do dote on me. It was a bit of a problem as I got older. Do you know I didn't have a boyfriend until I left for college? Brick and Jackson chased them all away.'

Plato relaxed. He liked these brothers of hers already. 'You don't say, Tex?'

'First thing I did when I got to Houston was check out the football team and get myself a quarterback.'

The tension shot back into his neck.

'Then Boyd turned up and threatened to have him thrown off the team if he had anything more to do with me. Boyd was a bit of a star on the university squad in his day, and the coach was a friend of the family, so…'

'No more quarterbacks,' he said with some satisfaction.

'I guess if I'd had a more normal romantic development I

wouldn't have taken up with Bill in the first place,' she said softly.

'When you overreact with me you're thinking about this guy who tried to control you,' Plato said in a deep dark voice, 'and it's made you wary. I understand.'

Rose lifted her head to protest, but he was right, and she found herself laying her head on his shoulder and confessing, 'I was supposed to be special to him. He was supposed to put me first before everyone else. Instead he put me last.'

'Rose.'

Plato's voice was rough. She could feel him looking down at her but she needed to get the rest of this out. Maybe it was the incredible intimacy of lying here with him like this, but she wanted to show him a little bit of her heart.

'I spent all my teen years finding matches for other people, watching other girls have romances. I wanted to have that for a change, and so I had to go behind my family's back to be with Bill. By the time I realised I'd made a mistake it was too late. I'd made my bed. I thought I had to lie in it. I was raised to honour my promises.' She looked up and met his eyes. 'It must sound crazy to you.'

'Honourable,' he said quietly, 'and young. You forget, I come from a small town. I know what it can be like.'

'Yes.' She sighed. 'And I wasn't the girl I am now.'

'Fiery, strong-willed.' He kissed her lips softly. 'My tough little Texan.'

'I was all those things before I met Bill, and then suddenly I couldn't be them any more. There was too much pressure on me not to be. To be someone else's version of Southern womanhood. In the end I just ran.'

'Ran?'

'To the shelter where I volunteered. They helped me organise myself so I could get the hell out of Houston.'

Plato's arms tightened around her. 'But not back to Fidelity Falls?'

'No. I was too ashamed.'

Plato said something in Russian. It didn't sound very nice. Then he pressed a fierce kiss to her temple.

It felt a lifetime ago at this moment, that life. She'd come so far. 'It was awful,' she said simply, softly. 'But it's over.' She angled up a curious look. 'Tell me about your family.'

'Just me and my grandparents.' He sounded gruff.

'Are they still alive? Do you go back and see them?'

'I go back whenever I can. The Wolves are based there.' He wanted to stop there, but she was shining those big blue eyes on him. He hesitated, then told her, 'My grandparents are gone now.'

'Did they live to see your success?'

'Nyet.'

The back of Rose's head nestled against his shoulder. He could feel her listening, her interest. What would it hurt to tell her more? To give a little of what she wanted?

'Dedushka—my grandfather—was born and lived under another system than the one I was able to take advantage of. He fought in the Great Patriotic War...'

'That's World War Two?'

'Da, it left him a broken man. They were poor. He didn't work. My grandmother ran the household. My mother fled the house at sixteen, came back a year later pregnant, desperate. They took her in.'

His voice had dropped an octave and Rose heard a wealth of meaning in those four words.

'Growing up, I barely saw her. She was never around. She—worked.'

'She must have loved you very much to make those sacrifices,' said Rose carefully.

'Da...sacrifices.' He laughed dryly. 'She drank, Rose. She worked hard and she drank it all away.'

She laid her hand on his bristly jaw. 'She must have had her reasons. I'm sure she loved you.' Something flashed through his eyes and Rose frowned.

'Da, she had her reasons. She liked the taste of vodka.'

'You don't believe that.'

He met her eyes, shrugged. 'It's not important now. She drank herself to death when I was fifteen. If you knew my grandmother you wouldn't have blamed her.'

Rose propped herself up, a little stunned by the cold smile on his face.

'There was a red corner in my grandmother's house—that's a place where icons are hung, to pray, and every night she would get down on her knees and beg the Lord to send the devil out of her house.'

Rose shuddered. She couldn't help it. Something passed across Plato's face—a look so painful Rose instinctively lifted her hand to his face, smoothed the silky hair off his temples, stroked. His grey eyes were stone-dark as they moved over her face.

'I'm sorry,' he said roughly. 'I don't mean to upset you.'

But he was looking at her as if he wanted something. More. From *her*.

Rose experienced a rush of soft feeling. She was going to have to tread very carefully, because she sensed this wasn't usual for him. Plato didn't strike her as a guy who spilt his guts. She'd grown up amongst taciturn ranchers, men who clenched their jaws and got on with it even when life dealt them unbearable blows. Plato Kuragin had tough Texan written all over him.

She cupped his stubbled jaw with the palm of her hand. 'Tell me…your grandmother was religious?'

'Crazy with it.'

Those thick brown lashes fanned down and she pressed a tender kiss to his temple. 'Why did she think the devil was in the house?' she asked quietly, reasonably.

His lashes lifted, and he fixed her with those unfathomable eyes. '*I* was the devil,' he said, in a low, rough voice. 'When she was done praying she'd get her broom and beat the demons out of me.'

Rose's hand slipped from his jaw. 'She would beat you—a child—with a broom?'

'Like Baba Yaga in the folk tales,' he said softly, then smiled thinly at her, 'Don't look so distraught, Rose. I wasn't home enough for it to be a regular thing.'

'How old were you when this started?' she whispered.

Plato saw the horror she was trying to hide in Rose's eyes and it hit him like a ton of bricks. What the hell was he doing? What was he looking for from this girl…? Comfort?

Da, get the princess to kiss it better for you and everything will make sense, a familiar cynical voice sneered.

'Where were you when you weren't at home?' she whispered.

In a criminal gang, running rackets for the local crime boss. 'On the streets. Getting up to mischief.'

Rose's eyes were full of concern, and Plato silently swore at himself. He didn't want to upset her, and he didn't want her pity. He didn't need it. Hell, in their Army days he and Nik had swapped childhood horror stories and some of Nik's had won hands down.

'I was a tough kid, Rose, but I've been luckier than most and I'm grateful for it. A local hockey coach noticed I had skills, put me in the junior league, got me off the streets, saved my life.'

'The Wolves?'

'*Da*, the Wolves.' Neutral ground.

'They're your family?'

He shrugged. 'Maybe. Yeah, if you want to look at it that way.'

Rose gazed at him steadily, then said, 'So how did you get from street kid to guy with big bucks?'

She was letting it go, and Plato could feel himself relaxing. He could paper over the rest. Instead he heard himself telling her the truth. 'I got a girl pregnant when I was seventeen. I was ready to marry her. I got a wedding coat and a job at the local mine. But she was smarter than me. She wanted out of that town, and she insisted we go to Moscow. I had this crazy idea it could work out—I'd do for my kid what my father had never done for me. But the truth was she just wanted the train fare. She had a guy in the city. There wasn't even a baby.'

'What did you do?'

'What do you think I did? I stayed. I took a chance, because there didn't seem much to go back for, and I built this life.'

'I understand. You did the only thing you could do,' murmured Rose, and she *did* understand.

When she'd left Houston she'd known there would be no going back to Fidelity Falls. Her four years with Bill had taken that possibility away from her. Changed her. You couldn't go back.

Rose settled her hands on his shoulders, brought her lips to his and kissed him. Gave him her understanding in the only way she knew. Because of that it wasn't a gentle kiss—it wasn't anything like that which had gone before.

Plato splayed his hand through her hair to deepen the kiss, rolling her under him to take what she was giving—and that was when he felt it. The force of what Rose held inside her, what she was communicating.

This wasn't just sex. Not for her, and certainly not for him. If this was just about sex he'd have had her four ways to Sunday, moving through his repertoire of positions and some of hers, until he was sated and she was telling all her girlfriends what a phenomenally good time she'd had. She wouldn't be outside his apartment before she started making calls…he was a trophy for women in this town.

Instead Rose had fallen asleep in his arms. Now they were eating in bed. Rose was asking him about his mother, his grandparents, and he was telling her. He was telling her things he hadn't revealed to another living soul. And now she was kissing him, and he was kissing her—not as a prelude to sex, although it was about to go that way, but because she wanted to share her feelings with him. And he was taking what she offered.

He lifted his head, looked down into her big blue eyes as he cradled her...

Since when had he cradled a woman in his arms?

The nimbus of her dark hair was drying around her face. He made a study of the classic contours of that face, those un-plucked dark brows of hers that just made her eyes seem more intensely blue, her mouth more ruby than red. She gazed back at him steadily, mirroring everything he felt...

What had he done to deserve all this?

Nothing. You deserve nothing.

Hell.

He needed to get this back to basics before he said or did something he would regret. He sat her up, disengaged her from his arms. Rose didn't seem nonplussed, but she was looking at him curiously.

He checked his watch.

'What is it?' she asked.

He thought fast. 'There's a party tonight, *detka*, how about we make an appearance? Introduce you to a bit of Moscow nightlife?'

He was getting off the bed. He was going to break up this little exercise in bonding with lots of people, lots of noise—a reminder of who he was and what she was doing here.

Rose didn't say anything. She didn't look hurt or confused or about to lose it with him. All she was doing was sprawling on the bed, incredibly sexy, bunching the sheet around herself, looking so at home Plato felt the muscles in his gut contract.

'What sort of party?' She didn't sound offended, merely surprised.

She didn't know.

'Opening night for a nightclub. I own it.' He forced him-self to smile, forced easy cynicism onto his lips, gave her the knowing look that made other women curl their toes. He knew what he was doing.

'Not the kind of nightclub I'm used to, I guess?' she said, watching him curiously.

'We don't plan on opening one in Toronto,' he observed with a wry smile. 'You'll enjoy it, *detka*. It'll be a circus.'

Rose turned up those druggingly sensuous blue eyes. 'What can I say? I love a circus,' she said with a little smile.

'*Horosho.* Good. I'll make a couple of calls, get you something organised.'

'Organised?'

'A dress…hair.' He made a gesture towards the masses drying over her shoulder, toppling down her back. 'Not that I wouldn't mind looking at it like that all night, but I don't think we'd make it out the door.'

It was supposed to be a compliment, something to ease the harshness of what he was doing, but Rose lifted one hand to her hair and for the first time looked uncertain.

Plato felt as if hooks had been lodged in his chest wall and just about now were pulling like crazy. He didn't think. He crossed to the bed, knelt beside her, turned up her face and kissed her.

He felt her relax, felt her arms lift around his neck. The sheet dropped and those gorgeous ruby-tipped breasts of hers rubbed up against his chest.

'Plato…' she sighed.

At this rate they weren't going anywhere.

'I can't believe you're organising me a dress,' she said, her eyes so blue, so close to his own, inviting him in.

'You can wear one of your own, but most of the women there will be in *couture*.'

'I understand.' She looked up at him, all eyes and sincerity. Her dimples came out.

Suddenly he didn't want to go to the party. But if they didn't he might very well start making plans with her—and he just wasn't that man.

It wasn't the right time in his life. Work had to come first. His lifestyle didn't support a girl like this. He couldn't give Rose what she needed.

So many reasons why not.

But he couldn't stop himself from saying, 'If you'd prefer to stay in...'

'No, you've got me in the mood now.' She snaked her way sinuously off the bed and gathered up her clothes. Her smile over her shoulder was pure Rose—all warmth and curiosity. 'But I should warn you, cowboy, I love to dance.'

CHAPTER FIFTEEN

ROSE was ready this time for the flare of cameras as their limousine drew up outside of the gates of a palace complex on an exclusive Moscow street.

Plato leapt out, his broad back to the paparazzi, thereby shielding her exit.

As he bent down to help her out of the car he said in a low voice meant only for her ears, 'You look incredibly beautiful. Have I told you that, *malenki*?'

Only a dozen times, thought Rose, thrilled.

In her long gown of dark blue watered silk with its embroidered bodice Rose *felt* beautiful—she felt like an eastern princess. She hadn't been sure when the stylist had shown it to her on a rack of similarly glamorous gowns, but with the right underwear it flowed over her curves like water down a ravine, pooling at her ankles. Her feet were clad in very high delicate heels and she wore a ruby pendant, nestled in her décolletage, and matching earrings.

When the cases of jewellery had arrived with an armed guard Rose had already been in the gown, and the temptation to accept the loan of the gems had been too high. But she couldn't stop the wandering of her hands to her throat and ears to check they were still there, and a couple of times Plato had smiled reassuringly at her when he'd caught her in the act.

He did it again now.

'Don't worry, *malenki*, it's just jewellery.'

Tens of thousands of American dollars' worth of jewellery, thought Rose a little faintly.

'It merely sets off what everyone is actually looking at.'

'This beautiful dress.' Rose held out her hem, giving it a sinuous shake.

'The woman wearing it,' said Plato, as if this was a fact that couldn't be questioned.

'You look very handsome yourself,' she said primly as she took his arm and dropped her chin to avoid the flash of the cameras as he led her rapidly into the building.

And he did. Plato and urban style got along very well.

For a boy from a small Urals town he sure knew how to dress—tonight in a mixture of central Asian design, even down to the tiniest detail of the way his blue *shalwar* trousers angled over the front of his very fine handmade shoes. He wore a *sherwani*—a long coat-style jacket—in midnight-blue, with satin inlays that just seemed to enhance how very masculine he was.

He smelt good too, of lovely exotic aftershave and clean male skin. He also had traces of her perfume on him from the car, which didn't hurt.

There were a lot of beautiful women converging on the club. Everyone seemed to know him.

It was like being on the arm of the Prince of the Underworld. This was where the beautiful people of Moscow came to play with him. And she was his date.

Rose held onto his hand as he led her through the well-heeled young crowd, past golden barred cages with go-go dancers, under crystal chandeliers that should have seemed incongruous, to a black and shiny seating area that was clearly exclusive given the four giant-size bouncers at the two entrances. They were on a mezzanine, high above the two dance floors, with deep sofas and ottomans and an Arabian Nights-esque feel that sent her sprawling against him as she tried to daintily take her seat.

Plato took prime position and seemed to take it for granted that she would just splay herself across him, as if he were some

Oriental potentate from another century and she was his harem girl. No, his much respected first wife, she corrected with a little smile as the heat from his big, hard body spread through hers. Rose tried not to enjoy it too much.

Other men gathered—business associates who did that European thing of kissing her fingers—and beautiful women, lots of women, who eyed her speculatively, summing up her dress, her hair, her jewellery, and then went back to watching Plato.

Plato made introductions, put a cocktail in her hands, and although the conversation began in English in deference to her it quickly lapsed into Russian.

Rose didn't mind. She watched the dance floor for a while, her body moving slightly to the pounding bass line. A guy sitting opposite leaned across and made the timeless gesture of an invitation to dance. Rose was about to agree when Plato's large body suddenly blocked her vision, forcing her to slide back as he leaned forward to say a few direct words to the other man. The guy was on his feet and moving away within moments. Plato eased back, sliding an arm around her shoulders, and then continued on with his conversation as if nothing had happened.

When Rose tried to get up his arm grew heavy around her.

'What is it, *detka*? What is it you want?'

She looked directly into his eyes. 'I'd like to dance.'

He placed a kiss in the curve of her throat and said in her ear, 'Later.'

Rose wasn't sure she liked the public kiss, coming as it did after the he-man tactics with the other guy and the possessive circle of his arm. It was all right for him to socialise, but she had to sit there with no one to talk to and nothing to do.

An accessory. After the fact of Plato.

That 'later' was not a winner either.

'Plato?' She made sure her smile was all big and shiny, telling him she was making an effort. 'I'll be dancing now, if you don't mind.' She took his arm and plucked it away from her shoulder, leaning forward to lift herself off the couch. 'If you're busy with your friends I can dance by myself.'

He moved so fast she was barely on her feet when his hand was around her waist. 'One dance,' he said.

He couldn't take his eyes off her.

It was a grounding realisation that at twenty-eight, having thought until now that he had seen it all, experienced it all, couldn't be shocked by much any longer, a blue-eyed Texan girl had taken his number.

He'd brought her to this party to neutralise her effect on him, to distance himself from what he had revealed about himself to her, and he'd only succeeded in intensifying it.

Rose danced with the same sensual abandon she'd brought to their bed. Her hips swayed, her arms moved sinuously over her head, her breasts grazed his chest—but she was locked in her own little world, special and private, as if there was a velvet rope between them and she wasn't going to invite him in. He wanted to take hold of it, rip it away, invade all that female mystery and…what?

He pulled her in close to him. Her eyes were shining as she looked up into his. It was impossible to be heard so he didn't bother with words. He just caught her mouth with his, taking what she would give so freely to him but needing to take it all the same. Needing her to know she was his, but he wasn't hers.

Rose emerged from the spell of the music and the rhythm to clutch at his steel-hard biceps as he ground his mouth into hers. He was bruising her lips, and it should have been awful, but a hot little spark darted through her and caught light and she writhed against him.

Plato swore in Russian and held her tight up to him, his mouth hot on her ear, 'We cannot have sex on a dance floor.'

'No,' said Rose, a little shaken. She wanted to tell him she'd never felt this way before, that this—everything between them—was moving so fast she was struggling to understand her own feelings.

This afternoon had started as a primal reaction to fear and violence and threat, and then it had become something else—something infinitely more personal, about her and him and the way it was between them, and sweeter because of it, more beguiling.

It was something else altogether in this place. He was another man here. The same man who had invaded her home that first night, the confident, take-no-prisoners guy who could only be accessed by an appeal to his libido.

She'd told herself this afternoon she had uncovered the Plato she had been responding to all along, the man who needed some tenderness in his life, the sort of comfort she knew she could offer him. But right now she wasn't so sure—and she was damn well spooked by her own response to him. Because her body seemed just as attuned to this arrogant sex god as it was to the man who cradled her tenderly in his arms. And didn't he know it?

As the crowd heaved around them and the music continued its insistent throb she realised being with Plato was not about hearth and home. He was purposefully opening up the distance between them. She could patently feel his regret at their intimacy, knew he was reminding her they were just about sex and nothing else.

She was never going to swan back into Fidelity Falls with this man, and he wouldn't be going anywhere with her...

This was all about right now, and right now it was all about sex and heat. They gazed at one another in unspoken accord. Plato moved first, his hand firmly around her waist, propelling her before him, literally surrounding her with the heat and protection of his body.

She saw him make a subtle gesture and suddenly a minder appeared in front of them and the crowd parted. Rose would have denied it under torture, but the knowledge he could do this, that with the snap of his fingers he could make things happen like this, sent a thrill suspiciously like sexual excitement through her body.

Plato moved with single-minded determination. The minder thrust open an exit door and suddenly they were alone in a narrow corridor.

'Where are we?'

He didn't answer. He just kicked open another door. And one moment she was standing in the corridor and the next she was up against a wall, and Plato was lifting her skirt and sliding his mouth over hers.

Rose didn't have time to think, only to react and her body was way on board. She opened her eyes only long enough to ascertain that they were alone, the door was shut, and then she fumbled for the buttons on his trousers.

'Rose, *moyu rozu.*' He was saying her name, crooning things in Russian that she couldn't understand, but somehow it aroused her, made her lift one bare thigh to bring him closer, to have him inside her.

She didn't understand what was going on between them, but this she knew. But with him. Only with him.

It couldn't be like this with anyone else for him either. She grasped his head between her hands and kissed him back fiercely, wanting him to know it was *her*, it was Rose, it was *his* Rose doing this to him.

He tore at the flimsy lace excuse she was wearing for panties and Rose felt her knees give with excitement. All she could think was that he would shortly be a part of her. They would be bonded. Nothing else mattered but this…

Voices in the corridor froze them. Plato's hand was on her inner thigh, and her fingers had spread firmly around him, guiding him…

'Der'mo,' Plato swore softly under his breath.

For a breathless moment her body was screaming at him to keep going, she didn't care that there were people just outside, and in that moment Plato seemed inclined to take this to its conclusion. Then his hand on her thigh shifted and she shuddered, gently biting down on his lip. He lowered her back against the wall, his hands going either side of her head as he leaned into her, breathing deeply.

Rose heard a door in the hall shut. Silence.

'We can't do this,' he muttered against her mouth, and she nodded, eyes shut, breath shuddering. 'Not here, baby, not now.'

'Rose. Call me Rose.' She opened her eyes and looked directly into his, because she'd known he was going to stop. That he *could* stop. Because he was in control and she was wildly out of control because this wasn't just sexual for her. This was her heart.

He's not going to love you, Rosy. You're lining yourself up for a terrible fall...

What did he see when he looked at her? A girl driven by her own libido or the real Rose, who needed to be in love to do this?

Yes, Rose, in love.

'Rose,' he acknowledged more softly, bringing a gentle, unsteady hand to her cheek, and what she saw in his eyes demolished what was left of her defences when it came to this man.

She'd been wrong all along. Love wasn't a decision made with the head—you couldn't arm people with information and skills and send them out into the world to make a choice about who you loved. She'd tried that once, with another man, and it had all gone to hell in a handbasket. Plato, in every conceivable way, was not the man for her, and yet...

When love happened to you it was a matter entirely out of your hands.

'Plato—'

She grabbed a fistful of his hair and pulled his head in, forging her mouth hotly to his.

If he had stopped her then she didn't know what she would have done. Begged? Kept going? Torn at his clothes? Yes, yes, yes—she would have done all those things.

She didn't have to. She felt the raw power of his lust slam her back against the wall. His hands closed over her bare buttocks, lifted her. The pulsing size of him was welcomed by her slippery heat and he was stretching her, and then he thrust, then thrust again, so deep she moaned despite her determination to be quiet, and he was moving inside her with a ruthless disregard for anything else but their pleasure.

He continued to kiss her, their mouths mating as their bodies moved together, her thighs clamped around his powerful lean hips. His grunts rose and fell in counterpoint to her helpless cries. She didn't even bother to be quiet. She wanted to wring every moment from this. And as she teetered on the brink of a climax Plato continued to drive inside her, muscles bunched in his shoulders as he kept her suspended between him and the wall. She broke apart and he slammed into her and came with a deep shout, his mouth hot at the base of her throat.

She pressed her brow to his, her breath coming in funny little gasps as she realised she was trying not to cry. Happy, victorious tears. He was hers and she could have him and she was woman enough to take what she wanted.

This was who she became when she was with Plato—this wild woman unafraid of her sexuality.

He let her down on her wobbly legs and pressed a fierce kiss to her temple. She could feel him trembling, his male skin slicked with sweat. Unable to help herself she pressed her face into his shoulder, suddenly overcome by the force of what they had done and what it meant to her, what she hoped it meant to him.

But Plato was pulling himself together. He smoothed his hand over the back of her neck, that gesture of possession and comfort she loved, but when she looked up at him she noticed there was a tension in his eyes that hadn't been there a moment before.

She stilled.

She wanted to tell him she loved him. It was all there, bubbling up excitedly through her chest, filling her mouth with silly, mushy words.

Instead she reached up and rubbed her thumb to the corner of his mouth, self-preservation throwing her a life-raft.

'Lipstick,' she whispered.

For a moment all she could see was his expression, the wild light in his eyes, and the regret in the tension all through his body.

As they re-entered the club, with the noise and press of bodies around them once more, Rose felt a little flutter of panic. She was going to lose him again. She turned to him a little desperately and pressed her mouth up close to his ear. 'When can we leave?'

'The night's young, *detka*,' he imparted, his gaze scanning over her head, avoiding making eye contact. 'Not yet.'

It was like a slap.

'I want to be alone with you,' she confessed, but he had already turned away, her words swallowed up by the music and the noise.

People were joining them. Rose was crushingly aware of how rumpled she looked—moreover that Plato was tattooed all over her skin. It would have been different if he had shown by a single gesture that this meant more to him than a sexual encounter, but she just knew now that he wouldn't.

He sat her down with a couple of other women, put a drink in her hand and said, 'I won't be too long—then we make tracks, *da*?'

She watched his retreating back as he vanished into the shadowy, light-swirling environs of the club—the shift of muscle in his back, his long lean grace. And that was when she knew. He wasn't coming back. Not the guy who'd showed up on her doorstep back in Toronto, making ridiculous accusations and all the while gazing at her with those hungry, baffled eyes. The man who'd whipped out her vacuum cord, driven her client down the stairs and told her she was coming to Moscow with him. That guy—the one who'd held her in his arms and made her feel hopeful and bold and special to him and him alone—was gone. She'd had her turn, and right now she was just another girl to him—a face in his crowd. He'd brought her here tonight to make sure she understood that.

She wasn't stupid. Part of her had known it even as she'd

put on her fancy dress, and she'd damned well known it when she'd forced him onto that dance floor. But she hadn't expected her own reaction to him, and even now the sexual feelings in her body were still surging, making it impossible to deny the raw edge to what was going on between them. If all this was only about sex for him, what did it say about her that she had been right along with him up against a wall? What did it say about *her* that she hadn't cared, had just wanted the excitement of being with him, thinking somehow, some way, she'd change his mind?

She'd known his reputation before she got into this. She had chosen to ignore it, decided she was going to be different. But how could she be when there was nothing different about any of this for him? Plato had been here before. She was the one who didn't know the score.

Oh, yes, she was the big expert on relationships. She'd ignored her own advice to other women. Advice that had been hard-won after four years under Bill's thumb. *You can't change him. Especially if he doesn't want to be changed...*

When Plato had told her about his mother and his grandmother, as a professional she'd understood immediately what it meant. He'd been starved of love by the two very women he should have been able to rely upon as a young child, and then had it taken away again by the putative mother of his child. It did much to explain the brevity of his relationships with women, the distrust. He was always waiting for it to be taken away.

She'd known then and there she'd taken on a lot more than a spoilt rich guy. But she didn't want to be his psychologist in this situation—she wanted to offer him up her heart and for him to protect it, just as she would protect his.

The unloved little boy he had been needed that, because God knew she had felt very much the same way as a little girl. But she knew the risk. The man he now was would very likely push her away. She just hadn't expected it to happen so soon, and she hadn't known she wasn't going to be able to handle it.

Because she'd been running from this very feeling since she was six years old. Being shut out of someone's heart. Except it was worse. She hadn't known it was going to feel worse.

The realisation that she didn't know what to do ripped through her as she stood up unsteadily to get a sight on him. He wasn't difficult to find—his height, his build, the way people got out of his way. She watched him approach a conclave of men at one of the bars. It was like watching meat being dropped into a pool of piranhas as women converged on him. Purposely, she reminded herself. He was doing this on purpose.

She almost expected it when a slender redhead, wearing not much more than a slip and skyscraper heels, slid her arm around Plato. It was when he shifted and casually encircled her waist that the glass in Rose's hand dropped from nerveless fingers, splashing the hem of her couture gown and rolling away. Because, deep down, she hadn't expected that.

Plato found Rose standing alone in the lobby, the pale curve of her back visible through the drapery of her midnight-blue gown.

It had taken ten increasingly frantic minutes to locate her. He'd almost gone wild, knowing Rose was somewhere in the club on her own—or, worse, outside of it. In those moments he'd regretted every stupid move he'd made this evening. He most regretted leaving their bed at all.

He took a harsh breath. Security were organising a car. He'd take her home. He'd make it up to her somehow. He'd explain... what? He wasn't worth her while. He didn't want her to get serious about him because he had nothing to offer her...

'Rose,' he said abruptly.

She turned. Her face was white, her ruby lips a taut line. She blinked those big blue eyes at him and he knew it was already too late.

'Rose?' The softening of her name came unbidden. 'Rosy?'

She gazed at him for a timeless moment. Her voice was hushed when she finally spoke. 'I saw you with the redhead.'

His coat slipped from his hands. He had been waiting to see the judgement in her eyes, had told himself it would right everything. Make crisp and clear and familiar what these emotions had made murky. Emotions he hadn't felt in years— longing, yearning, reaching for some softness in his life that just didn't seem destined to be his fate. But there was no judgement in those now familiar eyes. There was only pain.

'I did it on purpose,' he found himself confessing. 'Rose, do you understand? I did it to give you an insight into what it means to be in my life…'

She shook her head and uttered the little sentence he would have done anything in that moment to change. 'I don't want to be in your life any more.'

If she would only stamp her foot, round on him with her eyes snapping, hurl some charming, crazy country-girl epithets at his head until he was confounded and had no choice but to haul her back into his arms and not let her go….

But she didn't do any of that. She looked at him with those big blue eyes and he saw that at last the fire had finally gone out inside her. It was like a little death.

'Rose.' He could hear the desperation building in his voice. Damn it, was he going to *beg* her? What the hell was he doing? She was just a woman—easy come, easy go. 'I don't want this to be over,' he said, in a low, rough voice.

She stiffened, as if preparing for a blow. 'Will you come back to Toronto with me when this weekend is over?'

He frowned. Where had that come from? 'I have to be in London next week.'

Rose inhaled a sharp breath, as if he'd struck her.

'Come with me,' he said abruptly.

Rose closed her eyes. She could hear in his voice that he had surprised himself.

She waited for him to withdraw the offer, but he said more forcefully, 'Come, Rose.'

'I can't be with you, Plato,' she said, wondering why he was even bothering. Wasn't this what he wanted? 'Not like that. Your life is here, and my life is there. It's not going to work, is it?'

She couldn't believe how close this was to Houston. It was as if Bill's words were still ringing in her head: 'You wanted a husband and you came after me; you don't love me, Rose, and I don't love you, but you're hungry for love. Other men are going to come and go. I can accept that. I don't care as long as you're discreet.'

That was when she'd known she deserved more than what Bill Hilliger was offering. She'd known that then.

She knew it now.

She had gone after Plato and he didn't love her. He wasn't going to love her—not the way she needed to be loved—and she deserved more. The abandoned little girl she had once been deserved more. When she gave her heart it was going to be to a man who put her first. Before his grief, before his career, before himself—because she would do the same for him. In a heartbeat.

Rose slowly bent and picked up Plato's coat, feeling strangely heavy, as if every movement was an effort. She didn't want to hear any more. She just wanted to be left alone.

He closed the space between them so all she could see and feel and know was him. 'Let me take you home,' he said in a low voice. 'We'll talk, *malenki*, we'll sort this out.' He lifted a hesitant hand to her hair. 'I'm sorry.'

Rose shut her eyes. What was he sorry for? The redhead? For treating her like a face in his crowd? For bringing her here and making her think just for a little while…? Oh, yes, he really was the devil—temptation incarnate.

'Yes, take me home,' she said wearily. 'Take me away from here.'

In the car she sat as far away from him as possible, wrapped up in his warm coat. Yet still Rose felt her teeth begin to chatter. She was so cold. She'd never been so cold in all her life.

* * *

He rapped on the door. Hard.

He waited.

Rose had vanished into the guest room when they'd reached the apartment. He'd heard the door slam. There had been something about her that had made him hesitate to follow, so instead he'd gone and had a drink, then gone up the stairs and lain on the sheets where they had made love, where the scent of her was strongest.

A part of him asked, Wasn't it better to let it go like this? Whilst she was upset with him? Whilst she was riding that high horse of hers? If he pushed he suspected he could bring her down. She would still be wary but he could talk her round. And hadn't he taken her out tonight to destroy whatever little hopes she was building around him?

He remembered his grandmother spitting curses on his first visit home after a year in Moscow. A devil city. He would be corrupted. He wasn't worth half of his grandfather. It was his father's blood—whoever *he* was—which made him no good. *Go and don't come back*. He'd made his deal with the devil. He would have to live with it.

But he *had* gone back, and he'd given them what they would accept—all the stuff he could persuade his *dedushka* to take from him. Because a man in his eighties shouldn't be working in a field.

Just as a girl like Rose didn't belong in his world. He should just take her at her word and let her go.

He'd made his decision ten years ago, when he'd taken another girl at her word. He wasn't going back to that hick town with his tail between his legs. He was going to prove himself.

His grandmother was right. He'd made a deal with the devil, and here was the price.

Rose.

Rose, who'd given him one last anguished look coming into this apartment and turned her back on him.

His Rosy. She wanted the full picture—a husband, babies, a home. None of it was his to give her.

He'd let her sleep it off. Maybe he'd go down in an hour or so and find her, curl his body around hers and just sleep with her one last time…

Hell.

This couldn't continue.

He had launched off the bed and come carefully down the stairs. He didn't want to scare her.

He tapped on her door again. He said her name. Nothing. He rapped harder. Nothing.

So he eased the door open. The lights were off.

'Rose?'

Silence. He hit the switch. The bed was made. The room was still. Too still. He checked the *en suite* bathroom but by that time it was beside the point.

Her luggage was gone—and wasn't this what he'd wanted all along? Wasn't it?

CHAPTER SIXTEEN

SHE needed to keep busy.

Rose yanked her laptop out of her carry-on luggage and hit the power button. She hoped she had enough battery power left to see her through the next couple of hours.

Three days in the bosom of her family in Fidelity Falls and she was itching to get back to work, her friends, her life. It was crazy. All she had wanted to do as the taxi had taken her from Plato's apartment to the airport was see her family again. It had been her lodestar as she'd boarded the long-haul flight.

As soon as she'd hit the ground in Dallas and seen two of her four brothers, her dad and Melody waiting for her on the concourse she'd known she had made the right decision. She'd flown into their arms and put her tears down to having been away for over a year.

A day later she had been making arrangements to fly back to Toronto. She'd told Melody it was to do with the business— it wouldn't run itself. She hadn't mentioned that Phoebe and Caroline were doing a great job without her, and nor had she mentioned she'd cancelled all of her clients until next week.

It was true. You couldn't go back. Going home had just shown her how much she'd grown up. Her life wasn't in small-town Texas any more. It might not even be in Toronto, but she was standing on her own two feet and making her own decisions. This was her life—no one else's.

Her family had moved on with their lives. Her brothers

had families, her dad and Melody were planning a cruise next Easter, and around the dinner table she had been one of a crowd.

Her father had taken her aside and asked her if there was anything she needed, anything he could do. 'No, it's fine, Dad. I'm fine,' she'd said, and in saying it she had discovered she meant it.

Except for this weight on her chest that wasn't going to lift any time soon. This two-hundred-plus-pound Russian weight she knew she'd be carrying around for a while.

She needed to be like Phoebe—dating Sasha Rykov but keeping her head screwed on about it.

Who got serious about a twenty-four-year-old who had a slew of young women in Canada fixated on his every move right now? Sure, it was fun, Phoebe had said over the phone, but it wasn't going anywhere. It was neat to be the object of envy, and Sasha was very sweet. The sex was enthusiastic, and he seemed to think it was going to last for ever—but she knew it had a use-by date. Long before his contract with the NHL expired.

Rose tried to apply that wonky logic to Plato. He was a playboy billionaire. He flew in women the same way she ordered pizza. It was just one of those things. She'd had her fling. He'd been very clear. He wasn't going to move heaven and earth to be with her. He wasn't even going to pick up a phone and call her, ask her how she was…

She had visited her mom's grave on the way out of town. She'd laid wild violets against the headstone and told her about Plato and the awful truth that she had run out of ideas when it came to him.

'It seems I can fix everything else in this world, Mama, but I can't fix this man to love me. He's got other things he wants to do—namely blonde models.' She'd rolled her eyes as she said it, tried to make a joke of it, but it had fallen flat and she'd sighed. 'Plus I've got a business to run. I'm thinking I might take it nationally. I don't see why not. I don't see why I shouldn't aim as high as I can.'

Why shouldn't she aim high? She had nothing to lose. The laptop screen sizzled to life and she called up the Date with Destiny site. Time to get her head back into work space. It was the best cure-all. She could yell and stomp around and cry her heart out to her girlfriends—not in the middle of an economy flight en route from Dallas to Toronto, with a fat businessman to one side of her and a computer-game-playing teenager to the other.

She frowned as a photograph of the entire Wolves ice hockey team came up on their main page.

What the...? She scrolled down and combed through the text. Her pulse sped up, her face grew hot, and her foot began to tap against the chair in front.

She shoved aside her tender hurts, the painfully present knowledge that she would probably be a little in love with Plato Kuragin for the rest of her life...

Who the hell did he think he was, making a fool of her...?

'Here she is. Act naturally,' Rose heard Phoebe say in one of those exaggerated whispers.

She stepped over the ladder lying sidewards in the entrance and waved her hand around to dissipate all the dust. For a moment her anger was forgotten as she looked around at the disarray.

'How do you girls get any work done amidst all of this?'

Caroline, sitting at a makeshift desk behind a computer half-covered by plastic tarpaulin, said cheerfully, 'It's not so bad. Except when—'

A power drill started up and Rose cast a baleful glance at the handyman making holes in the wall. She flung her handbag over her shoulder and made a thumbing gesture outside. Neither of the girls was in all that much of a hurry to follow her, which pretty much let the cat out of the bag.

'What do you think of the office space. Pretty neat, huh?' said Caroline hopefully, gesturing at the building in general.

Rose gazed up at the pretty brick three-storey and had to admit it was lovely.

Then she levelled a mean look at her girlfriends and demanded, 'How much is he paying you, and how could you do this to me?'

'You've seen the website,' said Caroline with a sigh.

'Of course she's seen the website.' Phoebe put her hands on her hips. 'Cut the whining, Harkness. This is publicity gold for us. Twenty Wolves players, twenty dates, and a raffle. The money goes to the shelter and we go nationwide. If Plato Kuragin is feeling guilty about something, let him. Don't fight it.'

'I'm not taking anything from that man!' Rose declared, hating Phoebe because she was absolutely right.

'Too bad. Because we are.'

'Oh, Rose, whatever happened in Moscow, you need to move on,' said Caroline.

I haven't even dealt with it yet, thought Rose, a little disconcerted. This was the advice she gave on her website. *Keep moving. Don't look back.* Suddenly it seemed like the worst advice in the world. She'd expected sympathy from her girlfriends, not this practical 'we've got a business to run' from Phoebe, or 'get over it' from Caroline, of all people!

She stamped one foot. 'Why is he doing this?'

Phoebe put a hand on her shoulder. 'You're the only one who knows that, Rose. Look at it this way. You went to the Dorrington last week to get us some publicity and you got it for us—in spades. Don't look a gift horse in the mouth.'

'I swear,' said Rose, 'if he wasn't swanning around London right now I'd find him and plant a punch right in the middle of his perfect nose.'

Caroline was madly shaking her head and Phoebe grinned.

'What's so funny?'

'Big, rich and Russian isn't in London, babe. He's here in Toronto. Has been all week.'

It felt like a million years ago since she'd first stepped through the doors of the Dorrington Hotel, instead of merely seven days. She'd taken a chance on Plato being there, and as she walked across the lobby she caught sight of him in the bar.

Her heart stuttered.

It was impossible to miss him. Quite apart from his physically imposing size, he was simply the most gorgeous man in the room.

Her man.

She hadn't expected this—for it to happen to her all over again. She'd thought the sheer misery of it all would have killed those feelings, but instead they were stronger than ever. Her whole body was literally trembling.

As she came closer she noticed a couple of tables of preening women. All of them on parade. It was as if wherever he went there were girls making up to him. Paradoxically it brought her to her senses, and only served to make her madder.

Rose was suddenly very glad she'd slid her feet into her ruby heels this morning, donned her best blue woollen coat and collected her vintage bag—the one with the bird's wing clasp. She thought she cut a dashing figure. She was a girl about town. She had a ton more class than those floozies. Who drank in a bar at two o'clock in the afternoon? Okay, a posh, classy bar, but it was still a bar.

The same one she'd been dumped out of a week ago, on suspicion of solicitation...

Plato was leaning against the teak and gold railing with a group of other men. All shoulders, in a suede jacket spread open by the positioning of his arms to reveal the lean, hard-packed length of his torso. She recognised a couple of Wolves players. The other guys were older, with more flesh on them. They were listening to Plato.

Rose hesitated in the doorway and that was when he saw

her. His casual gaze caught on her, held, and he straightened up. For a moment he looked as stunned as she felt. Her heart stopped and he came towards her.

Her lover.

Pulling her bag in tight to her waist, Rose crossed the room with rapid little movements, shoulders back, working up her anger with every step she took and every step he no longer took. He just stood there, looking down at her.

At the woman who targeted him.

A fresh surge of anger pushed through her. *Right*. She would take care of this. She would make sure she was reasonable and low-key. She wouldn't let him see how much he'd hurt her.

'Why aren't you in London?' she demanded, the words just spilling out. 'Why are you doing this to me? Haven't you done enough? Haven't I paid a high enough price for daring to take a little publicity from you?' She stamped her heel, vaguely aware that this was neither reasonable nor low-key.

Why was he just staring at her?

'I'm sorry—all right? I'm sorry for being underhanded about it, but I was desperate. The shelter's lease was coming up and they needed the money. But you've solved that now. Which takes away my ability to be mad with you. So we've done our little bit of business, Mr Kuragin, and now I'd like to call it quits.'

She stuck out her hand and was proud of herself because it wasn't shaking.

Plato glanced down at her hand as if it were an unknown object.

Deep down she knew she was doing this all wrong. But she was desperately trying to hold on to her pride. She knew what he was doing here, standing in this bar, talking about the team and the game, pretending not to bask in the attention of twelve—count them—twelve women, all of whom would trample her just to get to him.

Back off, ladies, her subconscious snarled. *Mine.*

Shocked, she lifted unguarded eyes to his.

There were fine lines bracketing them. She'd never really noticed that before. But the expression in his eyes…there was something…

She hesitated, everything in her reaching towards him. But she knew everyone in the bar was looking at them, that she'd just done something very publicly that she really ought to have done with some decorum and class. But she was all over being well-mannered, and to her surprise she wasn't feeling any humiliation. She was feeling…

Hopeful.

Because he was looking at her as if…

Rose yanked herself away from the precipice. 'Good. Excellent.' She backed up on her heels.

She did the sensible thing, the only thing she could under the circumstances: she whirled around and stalked away.

Plato didn't move a muscle. Up until the moment Rose had walked into the bar he'd convinced himself that offering up the Wolves players *en masse* was going to be enough, staying on in Toronto until Sunday would be enough. Nothing was going to shift the selfish desire to go to her, to make her understand, to beg her…

And then she had walked into the bar.

For days he'd been unable to shake from his mind what had happened in Moscow. He'd taken her to that club to put a bit of space between them, to get his head on straight, to show her who he really was, to remind himself.

Da, the space. Other men looking at her, approaching her, trying to touch her had made him wild. He had barely been able to concentrate on anything other than keeping that space between them to a bare minimum. By the time they'd hit the dance floor he'd been unable to keep his hands off her.

He couldn't believe he'd dragged her into a backroom at the club, pushed her up against the wall and fallen on her like an animal. But it hadn't been mindless. Nor had it been about *This is who I am,* and *Look at how I'm treating you* any more.

It had been *This is what you mean to me. I need to show you what you mean to me.* As if what was pulsing between them had been starved and needed to be fed. But he hadn't understood then what it was…

The tabloids were full of his exploits—wildly exaggerated—and despite what he'd tried to convince Rose he didn't touch those women who hung around the clubs any more than he did the women who followed the team. From the start he'd always had an eye to his sexual health, and then there was basic male ego—who wanted to be with a woman who was interested only in your money or fame? But he'd wanted her to think that, hadn't he? He'd wanted to show her the worst, let her see what she was getting into…

Why he wasn't worth it.

Worthless. The worthless, illegitimate spawn of a worthless, promiscuous daughter.

That was when he'd known. When he'd been driving back from the airport—because he certainly hadn't let her go alone. He'd tailed her taxi to Domodedova, watched her from a distance until she'd vanished through check-in, and then he'd sat in the car and told himself to man up. To get over it. To understand he'd done the right thing, the only thing…

He'd left the apartment without security, so he'd driven away—not back to the apartment, but around the ring roads that encircled the city. Possibly one of the most dangerous things a man in his position could do.

But hadn't he been doing that all his life? Risking everything because deep down he didn't think he was worth it?

And he had known then why he had driven Rose away.

His entire life had been lived in opposition to the low expectations held for him. He'd built a financial empire, connections, a new family in the form of the Wolves, in spite of what his family, his town, sheer poverty had laid out as his future. Yet when it came to allowing a woman into his life he didn't have a clue. After all, the women who *should* have loved him hadn't considered him worth a skerrick of affection. Deep down he actually believed there must be a kernel of truth in those curses laid on him by a half-mad old woman long dead.

It was a stunning realisation to face and he'd been carrying it around for twenty-eight years. He hadn't seen it until Rose had forced him to face it. He'd spent the last decade pursuing empty sexual encounters and then he'd found Rose, with her open heart and soul. When he'd first gazed into her eyes he'd mistaken those feelings between them and her openness to him as a simple sexual connection, because it was the only currency between men and women he understood. But he knew better now.

Rose had been offering him a way into her heart, and he'd thrown it back in her face.

CHAPTER SEVENTEEN

'ROSE, you've lost weight, dear,' said Mrs Padalecki as Rose approached her front door, lugging the little suitcase she'd been beetling around with in her car all day.

'Have I?' She raised a smile.

'You look so thin about the face.'

'I've been off my food,' said Rose, truthfully enough. 'I'm sure I'll put it all back on over Christmas.'

She didn't want to stop and chat. She wanted to shut the door and be alone, as she hadn't been since she'd fled Plato's Moscow apartment three days ago. But Mrs Padalecki reached out across the low fence and Rose stepped towards her, taking her frail hand.

'How was Moscow? You weren't gone very long.'

'Wintry,' said Rose, 'and a bit overwhelming.'

Rita nodded as if she understood. 'He's not with you, then, that young man of yours? The foreign one?'

'Oh, no.' Rose affected a light laugh. 'No, I won't be seeing him any more.'

Rita's shrewd eyes moved over her face. 'That's a shame, Rose, he seemed—different.'

He was different all right.

Rose was surprised when Rita lifted her hand to her cheek. 'I can tell you cared for him, Rose.' Then the older woman shook her head. 'I will bring you in some food tomorrow and leave it in your kitchen. It's clear to me you're not eating properly.'

Rose didn't bother to object. She was having a great deal of trouble keeping the emotion lodged in a ball in her chest exactly where it was.

'I can tell you cared for him, Rose.'

Rita was the only person to acknowledge that. Caroline and Phoebe had called him all sorts of names over coffee. Phoebe had told her that off-hand, ridiculous story about Sasha over the phone, as if it wasn't obvious to everyone she was crazy about him. It was understandable. The people who loved her wanted to minimise the weight of the disappointment she was feeling.

Only seventy-two-year-old Rita Padalecki gave her the dignity of her true feelings.

I do care for him, thought Rose, as she closed her front door and leaned back heavily against it. *But I have my pride, and I'm afraid of my feelings if I let them loose and discover he doesn't care a spit for me.*

She was sitting at her kitchen bench when her cell buzzed. She was tempted to let it go, but in the end she picked it up.

It was Phoebe. She was at the Dorrington, organising the caterers for the after-party and lottery.

'You should be here, Rose. This is your baby. You grew this business. Your face should be the one people see tonight.'

Rose slumped forward onto her elbows. She couldn't go to the after-party. How could she admit to Phoebe she didn't want to see Plato? It made her sound so weak. She'd spent the last two years making herself strong.

But it was too soon. Her heart wouldn't stand it. He'd be there without a doubt, ruling the world, to pat her on the head and say, *There you go, baby, look how you've benefited from a night in my bed.* Or, worse, like this afternoon, he would say nothing because there was nothing left to say.

Because all it had been about was a weekend away with the girl of the moment.

She just hadn't realised that girl was her.

Pain did an assault course on her heart.

Rose shifted her cell to the other ear. 'No, Phoebes, I just can't.'

'I hate him,' said Phoebe vociferously. 'I've never seen you like this, Rose. What did he do to you?'

Made me want something I can't have. Gave me a glimpse of what it could be between us. And I got spooked because I've never felt this way before...so I quit first...but I'll never forget him...ever...as long as I live, because I think he was the one...

'He's just one of those rich guys, babe,' said Phoebe stridently. 'Probably never had to work hard for anything in his life.'

The man who'd given those boys from his hometown a way out and up. Rose opened her mouth to defend him, but Phoebe ploughed on.

'Let's take him for what he's giving and what we can get.'

What he was giving...

Rose almost dropped the phone.

He'd been in Toronto all week. She'd asked him to come and he had. She had been the one who had run. He had a lot of explaining to do, but she hadn't even given him the chance.

And now he was throwing stuff at her. Fixing things. Making it all right for her.

'Phoebe, I really have to go. Make sure the audio equipment is working. We don't want to get up on stage and not be able to be heard.'

'Yes, chief.' Phoebe paused. 'Did you just say you're coming?'

'Yes, it appears I am.'

Rose hung up abruptly. She didn't want to explain. She didn't even really have an explanation. But she needed to get into the shower and she needed a lot of make-up and she needed a killer dress.

She was over running away from him, and she was over judging him. For once she was going to trust him.

* * *

Plato only half listened to the question being directed at him by the bright-eyed young journalist, with her two cameramen bearing down on him as if he was an endangered species and they had him cornered.

The girl was saying something about the novelty value of tonight's stunt.

I am insane for agreeing to this, he thought wryly. *I should be across town, in Rose's little dolls' house, on my damned knees, begging for her forgiveness…*

'The proceeds are going to charity, it's promotion for the sport, and we've heard about how beautiful Canadian women are,' he drawled. 'Win-win, yeah?'

He'd said the right thing. Satisfaction crossed the hard face pushing a microphone into his space.

'Go and talk to the boys,' he said casually. 'They'll say the same thing.'

He knew they would because they'd all been schooled. He'd done it himself. This was his personal project.

The journalist gave him that speculative look he was accustomed to from women. She wasn't his type—too blonde, too skinny, too hard. But then a few days of dark and round and gentle as summer rain and he was ruined for life.

Was it only a week ago she'd stepped out of the scrum, blue eyes fixed on his face, that smile coaxing all sorts of outrageous thoughts to the surface of his mind? The same smile had dragged him across town on a wild chase after something elusive, something he'd found on that doorstep when fate had overstepped its bounds.

Rose.

There was a hush as a brunette in a deep amethyst sheath of a dress, which clung so tightly Plato swore if he was any closer he'd be able to see the indent of her navel, sashayed across the stage, microphone in hand.

'Ladies, gentlemen—if y'all would quieten down we can get this lottery underway.'

There was an almost immediate ripple of reaction across

the room. Nothing to do with the lottery, Plato recognised, and everything to do with the woman in the dress. It wasn't showing anything. It was a lot more modest than what most of the women here tonight had on. But there was something about the way she wore it. There was something about Rose.

His Rose.

Plato followed the purple satin from just above her breast to just below the curve of her sweet knees, so tight she couldn't be wearing a scrap of underwear underneath. Although he knew she was. He knew Rose would be wearing elaborate corsetry to ensure everything stayed exactly where she wanted it. In fact he could picture perfectly how that corsetry would look, snugly fitted to every last inch of her very female body. He just didn't want other men doing the same thing. Could they dim that spotlight?

'My name is Rose Harkness. I'm the director of Date with Destiny, and I'm honoured to be able to take part in this wonderful opportunity provided to us by the management of the Wolves ice hockey team. All proceeds tonight, as y'all know, will be going to a women's charity.'

She kept walking—swaying, really—as she spoke. The spotlight was barely keeping up.

She lifted her hand to shade her eyes. 'I'm sure he's out there somewhere, but Mr Plato Kuragin has been instrumental in bringing this to us, ladies, and I think he deserves a round of applause.'

Was it his imagination or was the top of that dress inching ever further south? At what point was he going to have to bound up there with his jacket to cover her up?

Why did she have people applauding him? This was *her* success, *her* moment. He'd engineered it all for her.

'Girls, y'all reach into those handbags, if you don't have your tickets handy already, because we're going to start lifting numbers. Where's that handsome Denisov? I believe he plays forward. Where are you, honey? Don't be shy!'

An hour. This was going to take at least an hour. An hour of

Rose, in that dress, with that voice, running her gentle hands over the boys as one by one they joined her on the stage. He would have to stand here in the dark, watching her flirt and manage and use those female skills of hers, until he went insane from wanting her, unable to tear his eyes away. Just like every other man in this room with a working Y chromosome. She actually had Denisov's arm around her waist. What the *hell* did he think he was doing?

Get your goddamn hands off my woman.

'Who is she?' asked Serge Ivanov, general manager of the Wolves.

'She's a pistol, whoever she is,' commented the guy beside him.

You can't take on all of them; maybe just land a punch on Ivanov.

'That's Rose,' said Sasha Rykov genially, tugging at his collar. 'Rose with the little gold pen.' He checked Plato. 'She's the Date with Destiny.'

Mine.

'*Da*,' Plato growled, 'she is.'

They circled one another for the longest hour of Plato's life: she running the show, he watching her back. His resolve was complete when he finally slipped out through the back of the hotel, formal attire shucked, the excited shrieking of two hundred women still ringing in his ears.

He went alone—no security. Just a guy in a suit, collar open, tie dangling, hands shoved into his pockets, keys jangling in his pocket. *Da*, it was a Porsche 911, but still, just a guy with an appointment. Across town. In the old district. Far from the noise and spectacle, the rush.

Rose had been giving an interview to the media when he left, all Southern charm and big blue eyes, holding them in the palm of her hand. She hadn't looked at him once.

But she knew he had left. Just as he knew she wouldn't be far behind him.

She wanted to call it quits? Like hell.

* * *

The light flickered on in her front room.

Plato, in his car idling across the road, had watched Rose climb out of a taxi, seen her fumbling in her bag at the door, and waited until he saw the light go on in her bedroom window. Then he'd killed the engine.

Now he jogged across the wet road, hands in his pockets, head bent under the force of the rain slicing down. He hadn't bothered with a coat, and by the time he stood at her door he was soaked. He rapped the lion's head door knocker and leaned his head against the frame.

No light came on, but presently he heard the locks rattling, and the door cracked open. The hall was down-lit behind her, but he could make out the shape of her face, the curve of her shoulder. Rose kept the security chain in place.

She looked up at him, her hand still on the handle, as if at any moment she was going to slam the door in his face.

'Rose.' Her name came out hoarsely, as if his throat had been scraped too many times from saying it.

Then slowly she lifted the chain, opened the door and let him in. He shouldered it shut behind him on the night and the rain and the rest of the world.

Her big blue eyes were turned up to him. She didn't say a word. She'd removed the purple dress, was wrapped in some sort of ivory silk robe. Her hair was down; her feet were bare.

He was about to speak but then Rose was in his arms, dragging his head down, pushing her mouth up against his. Her mouth was so soft, but she was angry. He could feel the force in her, found himself answering it.

She began pounding on his chest with her fists and he let her. Then she went quiet, her hands spreading, her body quaking, and the face she turned up to him was wet with her tears. He burrowed his head in her neck, fisted his hands in the silk over her hips. He was backing her towards the stairs. She hooked her arms around his neck and he lifted her, carried her, unerringly found his way to her bed.

He fumbled with all the hooks and eyes. She was wearing

some sort of restrictive corset of a garment and he wondered
how she could breathe in it. It had left tiny red welts on her
pale skin, and he fell to tracing them with his thumb, his lips,
his tongue, smoothing out the marks across her breasts and
belly and hips. As if he could make better what had hurt her.

When she lifted under him he thrust inside her, and they
found a rhythm, old as time, that rocked them through the questions of why he was here, how she'd known he would come,
and why nothing else mattered. Rose answered by forging her
mouth to his, taking what she wanted, and he gave it to her, the
muscles bunching in his upper back and then in his quads as he
lifted her upright with him. Rose straddled him in the centre
of her rickety double bed, cleaving to him, coming apart in his
arms. She collapsed on top of him, and he could feel the rise
and fall of her heavy breathing as she began to sob.

'It was a *coup de foudre*,' he muttered hoarsely into her
messy hair, 'and I fought it, Rose. I had to.'

'Why?' she sobbed.

'Because I knew what it would mean. I'd have to give it
all up.'

Her head lifted. Her eyes were huge, drenched. 'Give up
the other women?' The words came painfully from her throat.

He looked at her almost wildly, catching her face between
his big hands. 'No. There *are* no other women. Don't you see,
Rose? It was never about other women. It was me. The self-
loathing, the despair. To be with you I'd have to finally believe
I was a better man.'

Rose heard the echo of what she had said to him, but seeing the pain in his eyes was what convinced her and it stunned
her into silence.

Plato gently disentangled their limbs, only to draw her into
his arms, cradling her against him. His voice was very low and
still hoarse when at last he began to speak. 'I built this life for
myself—cold, hard, soulless.'

'No.' Rose caught his face with her hand, made him look
at her. 'That apartment of yours in Moscow—that was soul-

less. I walked from room to room thinking. This must be who he is. This is the man I could be falling for. How could I be so wrong?'

Plato drank in her face, seeing beyond the delicate, lush features to the person she was.

She regarded him solemnly. 'When I saw that ridiculous entertainment console—that's when I thought maybe we had a chance.'

Plato laughed desperately, pressing his forehead to hers. 'I almost lost you,' he said roughly.

'Then we found each other again,' she reminded him, her eyes so big and blue and shiny.

'I didn't feel I deserved you.'

Rose shook her head in wonder.

She needed to hear the truth, however painful, and Plato knew he had to give it to her.

'All along I've been telling myself this couldn't work. In Moscow I took you to that club to show you what I was, but it was you who showed me. I didn't like what I saw, Rose, and Moscow without you was empty. London was too far away. I came to Toronto to make things right for you. I had no intention of trying to heal things between us. I thought you were better off without me.'

Rose touched his face.

'I didn't feel worthy of being loved. By anyone, let alone you. You've brought something softer, something decent into my life, Rose, and I've never had it before. Forgive me for not recognising it.'

'You love me?'

'I've loved you from the moment I saw you, Rose,' he said with simple formality. 'I just didn't have the ability to recognise something I'd never known.'

Rose gazed at him wonderingly.

'It's the same for me. I thought love was like my college degree. You just put in the work and you got a diploma. I'm such a fraud. If my clients had any idea how little I actually know...'

'We will have to remedy that,' said Plato, sounding much more himself, with that smug male note back in his voice. 'The wine is drunk, Rose.'

She angled an amused look up at him. 'And what's that supposed to mean?'

'It's an old Russian saying. It means there's no going back. You're already mine. The wedding will be a formality.'

Rose sat up on her forearms. 'Are you proposing marriage to me, Plato Kuragin?'

'I will be—at the appropriate time, with the appropriate jewellery.'

Rose buried her face in his chest hair. She really did love it. But Plato was sitting up, dislodging her. She realised what he was doing as he reached out for her corselette hanging off the end of the bed.

'You answer the door wearing this?' He sounded more accusatory than amused as he dropped back onto the pillow, slinging an arm behind his head and propping himself at an angle, the better to slide her in against him.

'Only to you,' she answered primly, amused when he restored her head to his chest. He really was incredibly old-fashioned, for all his reputation...

'Plato?' she murmured.

'Rose?' he replied with a smile in his voice, twirling the white Spandex and satin confection in one hand.

'I've been meaning to ask you... I read somewhere...'

'In a tabloid?'

'Maybe. The orgy on the super-yacht...?'

'Rose, that never happened.'

She subsided happily back against his chest, not realising until this moment how much it had been bothering her.

Although he *had* answered rather quickly...

'What are they going to do, with you all happily married and living in Toronto?'

Plato relaxed under her, as if the thought was a pleasant one. 'Find some other poor guy to torment.'

'I don't know.' Rose grinned. 'Maybe they'll start writing about me. I can be pretty wild, you know. I've even been known to pick up and fly off to Moscow at a moment's notice with a sexy Russian billionaire.'

'*Da*, in your single days, *malenki*. That's all over. Now you pick up and fly off to the Maldives with your sexy Russian husband.'

'I haven't said yes yet, cowboy.'

He lifted her chin, nudged her dimple. 'Rose, will you be my wife?'

'*Da,*' she whispered, and closed her eyes as he kissed her. When she opened them Plato was gazing at her, and she could swear he looked a bit misty. Her big, tough, invincible Russian.

He was a romantic after all.

'I just thought of something,' she said. 'Mrs Padalecki.'

Plato looked mildly surprised. '*Da*, what about her?'

'I want to tell her first. Our news. After all, she's almost family.'

Plato chuckled, that lovely rumbling sound deep in his chest, and Rose spread herself happily out over him. His hands began to wander.

'We will tell her later, Rosy. Much later.'

* * * * *

ROMANCE

Contract with Consequences	Miranda Lee
The Sheikh's Last Gamble	Trish Morey
The Man She Shouldn't Crave	Lucy Ellis
The Girl He'd Overlooked	Cathy Williams
A Tainted Beauty	Sharon Kendrick
One Night With The Enemy	Abby Green
The Dangerous Jacob Wilde	Sandra Marton
His Last Chance at Redemption	Michelle Conder
The Hidden Heart of Rico Rossi	Kate Hardy
Marrying the Enemy	Nicola Marsh
Mr Right, Next Door!	Barbara Wallace
The Cowboy Comes Home	Patricia Thayer
The Rancher's Housekeeper	Rebecca Winters
Her Outback Rescuer	Marion Lennox
Monsoon Wedding Fever	Shoma Narayanan
If the Ring Fits...	Jackie Braun
Sydney Harbour Hospital: Ava's Re-Awakening	Carol Marinelli
How To Mend A Broken Heart	Amy Andrews

MEDICAL

Falling for Dr Fearless	Lucy Clark
The Nurse He Shouldn't Notice	Susan Carlisle
Every Boy's Dream Dad	Sue MacKay
Return of the Rebel Surgeon	Connie Cox

0712 GEN STD HB

Mills & Boon® Large Print

August 2012

ROMANCE

A Deal at the Altar	Lynne Graham
Return of the Moralis Wife	Jacqueline Baird
Gianni's Pride	Kim Lawrence
Undone by His Touch	Annie West
The Cattle King's Bride	Margaret Way
New York's Finest Rebel	Trish Wylie
The Man Who Saw Her Beauty	Michelle Douglas
The Last Real Cowboy	Donna Alward
The Legend of de Marco	Abby Green
Stepping out of the Shadows	Robyn Donald
Deserving of His Diamonds?	Melanie Milburne

HISTORICAL

The Scandalous Lord Lanchester	Anne Herries
Highland Rogue, London Miss	Margaret Moore
His Compromised Countess	Deborah Hale
The Dragon and the Pearl	Jeannie Lin
Destitute On His Doorstep	Helen Dickson

MEDICAL

Sydney Harbour Hospital: Lily's Scandal	Marion Lennox
Sydney Harbour Hospital: Zoe's Baby	Alison Roberts
Gina's Little Secret	Jennifer Taylor
Taming the Lone Doc's Heart	Lucy Clark
The Runaway Nurse	Dianne Drake
The Baby Who Saved Dr Cynical	Connie Cox

0712 GEN STD LP

Mills & Boon® Hardback
September 2012

ROMANCE

Unlocking her Innocence	Lynne Graham
Santiago's Command	Kim Lawrence
His Reputation Precedes Him	Carole Mortimer
The Price of Retribution	Sara Craven
Just One Last Night	Helen Brooks
The Greek's Acquisition	Chantelle Shaw
The Husband She Never Knew	Kate Hewitt
When Only Diamonds Will Do	Lindsay Armstrong
The Couple Behind the Headlines	Lucy King
The Best Mistake of Her Life	Aimee Carson
The Valtieri Baby	Caroline Anderson
Slow Dance with the Sheriff	Nikki Logan
Bella's Impossible Boss	Michelle Douglas
The Tycoon's Secret Daughter	Susan Meier
She's So Over Him	Joss Wood
Return of the Last McKenna	Shirley Jump
Once a Playboy...	Kate Hardy
Challenging the Nurse's Rules	Janice Lynn

MEDICAL

Her Motherhood Wish	Anne Fraser
A Bond Between Strangers	Scarlet Wilson
The Sheikh and the Surrogate Mum	Meredith Webber
Tamed by her Brooding Boss	Joanna Neil

Mills & Boon® Large Print

September 2012

ROMANCE

A Vow of Obligation	Lynne Graham
Defying Drakon	Carole Mortimer
Playing the Greek's Game	Sharon Kendrick
One Night in Paradise	Maisey Yates
Valtieri's Bride	Caroline Anderson
The Nanny Who Kissed Her Boss	Barbara McMahon
Falling for Mr Mysterious	Barbara Hannay
The Last Woman He'd Ever Date	Liz Fielding
His Majesty's Mistake	Jane Porter
Duty and the Beast	Trish Morey
The Darkest of Secrets	Kate Hewitt

HISTORICAL

Lady Priscilla's Shameful Secret	Christine Merrill
Rake with a Frozen Heart	Marguerite Kaye
Miss Cameron's Fall from Grace	Helen Dickson
Society's Most Scandalous Rake	Isabelle Goddard
The Taming of the Rogue	Amanda McCabe

MEDICAL

Falling for the Sheikh She Shouldn't	Fiona McArthur
Dr Cinderella's Midnight Fling	Kate Hardy
Brought Together by Baby	Margaret McDonagh
One Month to Become a Mum	Louisa George
Sydney Harbour Hospital: Luca's Bad Girl	Amy Andrews
The Firebrand Who Unlocked His Heart	Anne Fraser

0812 GEN STD LP